Tag Against Time

TAG
AGAINST
TIME

HELEN HUGHES VICK

Harbinger House

BOULDER, COLORADO

Harbinger House appreciates the helpful guidance from
Platt Cline and Richard K. Mangum, noted Flagstaff
historians, and Connie L. Stone, professional
archaeologist, in the preparation of this book.

Harbinger House, an imprint of
ROBERTS RINEHART PUBLISHERS
5455 Spine Road, Mezzanine West, Boulder, Colorado 80301

Manufactured in the United States of America
This book is printed on acid-free, archival quality paper.
Designed and typeset by Whitewing Press / San Francisco
Cover illustration by David Fischer

2   4   6   8   10   9   7   5   3   1

Library of Congress Cataloging-in-Publication Data
Vick, H. H. (Helen Hughes), date
Tag against time / Helen Hughes Vick.
p.   cm.
Sequel to: Walker's journey home.
Summary: Twelve-year-old Tag struggles with himself and encounters
historical figures and events as he time-travels from the ancient
cliff-dwellers period to the present.
ISBN 1-57140-006-0. -- ISBN 1-57140-007-9 (pbk.)
[1. Time travel--Fiction. 2. Hopi Indians--Fiction. 3. Indians
of North America--Arizona--Fiction. 4. Walnut Canyon National
Monument (Ariz.)--Fiction.] I. Title
PZ7.V63Tag   1996   [Fic]--dc20   95-45371

To my own
Michael T.
and
Lauren Marie

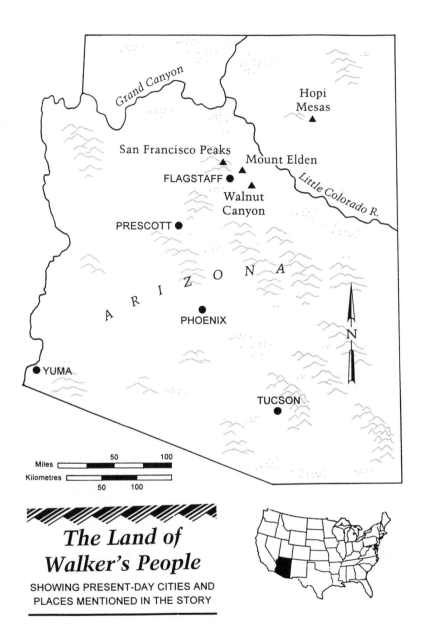

The Land of Walker's People

SHOWING PRESENT-DAY CITIES AND
PLACES MENTIONED IN THE STORY

1

The twelve-year-old boy's freckled face was streaked with time. His curly brown hair was matted with the ages. He drew up a gangly leg and reached down to tie his fluorescent shoelaces. His feet felt pinched and cramped in the heavy jogging shoes. He fingered the handwoven yucca sandals that lay next to him, and said to himself, "It's going to be hard to get used to wearing real shoes again." Tag tucked the sandals next to the leather loincloth on top of the other clothes in the old canvas backpack.

He picked up the small ceramic canteen, shaped like a tortoise shell, rounded on one side, flat on the other. Tag pulled the wooden stopper from the small opening at the top. "Better take a drink now since I don't know how many years it will be till I get another one." Would the water in the canteen evaporate during time-walking? Tag chuckled. Now that was an interesting thought. What could scientists learn about A.D. 1200 from just a few drops of water? He wedged the stopper back in tight. "Of course, I have plenty to tell them—but will they believe me? Will even my own dad believe me?"

Tag shook his head and laid the canteen on the top of the backpack. Buckling up the pack, he knew that what he had lived through was inconceivable. He hardly believed it himself.

His knees creaked as he got up. Tag shook his long legs to get the pant legs down to where they belonged. The stiff, blue jeans chafed his sun-baked skin. How could he have ever thought that jeans were comfortable? Maybe he'd put his loincloth back on. It was less restrictive than his old clothes or were they his *new* clothes? Tag laughed. Time was relative. He slung the pack onto his shoulder. What would Mom and Dad think if he came home to the nineteen-nineties wearing nothing but a seven-hundred-year-old Sinagua Indian loincloth?

A flash of lightning outside lit up the small cave.

He stooped down and picked up an eight-inch-long, leather-wrapped object from the cave's limestone floor.

Thunder rolled into the cave vibrating the close walls.

Tag unwrapped the soft folds of buckskin. Sweat formed on his forehead as he looked down at the fragile prayer stick. A thin strand of leather tied the two distinctive pieces of wood together. Each piece of wood had a carved face, the left a male, the right a female. The white eagle feathers adorning the ancient images fluttered in the breeze that was drifting into the cave's opening.

How can such a primitive object have such immense power? Tag wiped the sweat out of his eyes. The carved wood of the paho felt as fragile as fine glass. The feathers looked as though one strong breath of air would disintegrate them. Yet his future lay within this ancient prayer stick. A chill slithered up Tag's spine and pulled at the tight curls on the back of his neck.

The future...

Tag looked around the small cave. Standing in the middle, he could almost touch each wall. The cave was only a few feet deep. At five feet, seven inches, Tag had to duck to get inside its low entrance. This small, unremarkable cave was the aperture into time; the ancient paho, the key that opened the passageway into the future.

Lightning lit up the cave for a split second.

The future...

Clutching the paho, Tag's thoughts flashed to the afternoon when his incredible journey began. That afternoon was now seven-hundred-odd years in the future. Tag closed his eyes. His memories of that day were vivid and clear as his mind relived scaling up the ten-foot-high cliff to the cave. Lightning had been striking all around him. He had just known he was going to get fried at any minute. His heart echoed the roll of thunder as he pulled himself over the top of the cliff. Rain drenched his face.

He scrambled across the narrow stone ledge to the cave's low entrance. Lightning struck a pine tree just to the side of the cave. Tag dove into the cave's dark entrance. An overpowering, blue light surged through the cave. He saw an Indian boy bending over a pile of rocks at the back of the cave, holding something in his hands. The cave exploded with thunder and darkness. In that instant of darkness, his life had changed forever.

Tag remembered regaining his senses and finding Walker, a fifteen-year-old Hopi, in an unconscious heap. He cringed

3

at the memory of his brassy interrogation of Walker. How could he have been so rude—no, just ignorant of the Hopi ways?

Pushing away the uncomfortable memory, Tag guided his mind to the moment that they had left the cave. He relived the shock of seeing the canyon. Despite the fact he had lived on its rim for five years, the canyon was alien. The once heavily-vegetated canyon was now parched and dry. Even the air felt different; crisper, cleaner—hostile.

"We have walked time—walked back to when the ancient ones lived in this canyon," said Walker, staring down into the canyon. "I was sent here for a purpose and for some reason time is running out." They sat on the ledge outside the cave. Walker explained that he came to the cave because of his Uncle's Náat's dying request to, "Do what must be done." Walker looked over at Tag. "Things could get dangerous. Maybe you should stay here in the cave while I go..."

"No way, buddy. I'll just keep tagging along with you. Excuse the pun."

Tag let the memories of their incredible and dangerous adventure of living with the ancient ones fast-forward in his mind, as the thunder echoed outside the cave. Great Owl, the seer and powerful magician, had given them shelter and spiritual guidance. White Badger, Great Owl's son, gave unquestioning friendship and protection. Tag's stomach growled at the memory of Morning Flower's unusual but tasty meals eaten by Great Owl's fire pit. He smiled at the thought of Flute Maiden's pretty, oval face, and deep, slanted eyes. Did Walker see the love revealed in her eyes?

The memory of four-year-old Small Cub's laughter filled Tag's mind with love and worry. Small Cub had become like a little brother to him. Could Small Cub survive the sickness that brought swift and certain death to the inhabitants of the canyon?

Please let Small Cub live, Tag prayed. *Please...*

Gray Wolf's thin, angry face seared through Tag's prayer. "Witches. They are two-hearted witches. Kill them now before they bring death to all of us!" Gray's Wolf's voice screeched through Tag's memory.

Tag's mind jolted back to the cave as his eyes flew open. His scalp tightened. Like turning on a light after a nightmare, a brilliant flash of lightning illuminated the cave. Tag struggled to get control of himself. The holy paho shook in his clenched hand. How had they ever survived Gray Wolf's deadly intentions?

Thunder shook the walls of the cave.

Tag tried to steady the shaking paho. His knees felt like rubber, while his stomach twisted in tight leaden knots. He was safe from Gray Wolf, but would he ever feel truly safe again? What real nightmares did the future hold for him? Tag attempted to swallow the tightness in his throat. Had he made the right decision to try to time-walk back to his own place in time? There was no guarantee he could even get back to the nineteen-nineties. The tightness in Tag's throat moved upward. His chin trembled. Would he ever see Mom and Dad again? *If only Walker were coming with me,* Tag shifted the paho to his other hand. No, Walker's decision to remain behind with the ancient ones was correct. The ancient ones were *his people*, his flesh and blood.

Tears blurred Tag's vision. He reached up and wiped his eyes. Worry nagged like a canker sore. Could Walker lead his people out of the death-filled canyon and guide them to a new home on the Hopi mesas far to the northeast? What were the odds that anyone would survive such a long journey in A.D. 1200 and something?

It's still not too late. Tag looked toward the cave's opening. *I can climb down to the village and tell Walker that I've changed my...*

"My son, now is the time for you to do that which you were sent to do." Great Owl's words filled the cave as if they were thunder.

Tag whipped around searching the cave even though he knew he was alone. Was Great Owl seeing his thoughts? Would Great Owl watch his every moment through time? The assumption gave Tag a curiously comfortable feeling. But what did Great Owl mean? "Now is the time for you to do that which you were sent to do." What was he supposed to do? What could he do? Confusion compounded Tag's apprehension. *How will I ever know?*

Lightning flashed outside. Its brilliant light illuminated the cave for a split second. The paho seemed to absorb the light and its power. Tag felt a strange and wondrous energy radiating from it.

"You must think good thoughts—positive thoughts; our great creator, Taawa, will guide your steps." Great Owl's words were thunder. "Place the holy paho on the shrine."

Tag's heart beat against his ribs as if it was trying to escape. Whether he wanted to or not, Tag knew he had to walk into the future. His time with the ancient ones was over. The rock shrine sat on a natural shelf protruding from the cave's wall. Tag took a deep breath and held it.

Good thoughts, happy thoughts—pepperoni pizza, juicy hamburgers, curly french fries—soft, clean beds, flushing toilets, hot showers. Tag placed the holy prayer stick on the shrine. *Mom, Dad...*

A dazzling, blue light filled the cave. In the same instant the cave exploded with thunder. The deafening sound echoed through Tag's head, piercing his brain with pain.

Total darkness consumed the cave. The air felt heavy with age, decay, and death. Thunder vibrated through Tag's body. He slumped to his knees, gasping for air. None would come.

The cave swirled and twisted in time...

2

The cave ceased twisting and turning. Time stopped.

Tag tried to get his leaden eyelids open, but couldn't. His head throbbed in pain as warmth thawed his cold body. The rocky floor of the cave gnawed at his back. He managed to roll over onto his side. The glaring light beat against his closed eyelids. Tag fought to bring his mind into focus.

I'm still in the cave, but where—no, when *am I in time?* He knew it could be anywhere from A.D. 1250 to infinity. *But when?* Fear and uncertainty again began building in the pit of his empty stomach. Had he been wrong in leaving Walker and the ancient ones? His stomach knotted in hunger. *No,* it growled. Tag's mind agreed even in its unfocused, floating state. Although he had made lasting ties with the ancient ones, his true bonds were with pizza, computers, and running water. Tag's heart interjected; Mom and Dad. Living with the ancient ones made him realize how much a part of his parents he was.

Before his journey back into time, he resented the long hours his father, a field archaeologist, spent studying, "dead Indians." Pain thundered through his head. *How could I have been so childish?* Tag now understood his father's deep-seated desire to learn about the ancient ones and help preserve their culture. He could hardly wait to apprise his dad about what it was really like to live with those who held his fascination. The stories he had to tell!

If I ever see Dad or Mom again, Tag's mind focused sharply now. Tears stung behind his closed eyes as his heart merged with his mind. His mom's freckled face, her smiling brown eyes, and wild curly hair, flashed through his mind. Tag clenched his eyes tighter, trying to see her face better. A baseball-sized lump filled his throat. "You're a twelve-year-old going-on-twenty," her often spoken words resounded through his memory.

I might act twenty, but I'm still a kid! his heart screamed. *And I want to go home!*

Hot tears burned his check. Great Owl promised that he could try more than once to get back. *But how many times? Two, three, five, twenty-five?*

The cave's floor was getting harder by the second. He had to move or petrify lying there. It was time to face reality, whatever or *whenever* that was. Tag forced his eyes open. Sunlight washed the cave. The air felt uncomfortably warm.

The paho lay on the stone shrine. "Remember, my son, the paho only has power when the moon illuminates the passageway of time." Great Owl's words echoed through Tag's mind as he struggled to his feet. His bones cracked as if he had lain in one position for years. He groaned. The groan echoed off the cave's close walls. Tag jumped, looking around. Realizing what had happened, he laughed. The sound bounced around the cave, laughing with him.

Tag reached for the ancient paho, his key to time. "I'd better keep this with me every minute. If I lose it, I'll never make it home." His words repeated themselves as he reached for Walker's backpack laying nearby.

"Walker of Time, where are you walking now? How many of your people are walking with you?" Tag whispered, wrapping the prayer stick in its buckskin. An ache rose in his throat. Walker's handsome, reddish-brown face, with its high forehead, and dark, slanted eyes streaked across Tag's memory. Would he ever know what happened to his friend? He chuckled. "I know. I know. It's rude to ask so many questions. It's not the Hopi or the ancient ones' way to ask questions."

Tag noticed the small natural basin below the shrine that had been formed by years of water seeping through the limestone. When he left Walker, it was half full. Now, it held only a fingertip of water.

"Proof! I have gone through time." A surge of excitement shot through Tag. "But how much?"

His voice echoed back the question. Maybe he was back in 1993 already.

"Let's go find out." Tag answered himself. He placed the prayer stick on top of the pack.

"Go find out. . .Go find out," his hollow echo tolled through the cave.

Like an oven being opened, hot dry air blasted Tag as he stood on the narrow ledge in front of the cave. He gazed down into the rocky, six-hundred-foot canyon. "I can't believe it," he whispered. "Things are even worse than when I left."

10

The drought that baked the ancient ones' crops in the fields and dried up their limited water supply had worsened. What little sage and bee grass that had been growing on the canyon sides were gone. Cacti were the only living things now, and they even looked wilted beyond revival. The rugged crags and crevices of the canyon stood hostile and barren in the glaring sun.

What else had changed? Deadly silence permeated the canyon. Tag looked down the sheer, ten-foot-cliff he'd have to descend to get to the village. The memory of his close call the first time he climbed down it, sharpened his apprehension.

Obviously, I'm not back to my own time. I don't have to go down, I can just go on into time.

A raven's shrill cry echoed in the canyon.

"Now is the time for you to do what you were sent for," Great Owl's words replaced the raven's call in the scorching air. Goose bumps rose on Tag's arms.

He plopped down on the ledge of the cliff, letting his long legs dangle in midair. The heat from the limestone seared through his jeans.

The old proverbial hot seat. Of course, he had to go down into the village. The part of him that was his father, the archaeologist, the lover and studier of peoples, wouldn't allow him to take the easy way out. He had to see, to experience what the village was like now, whenever that was. He yearned to be a part of the living history of Walnut Canyon so that he could tell his father all about it.

By the look of things, Tag had a gut feeling that the vandals and pothunters had not yet done their dirty work of destroying and stealing time. His heart thundered at the thought of grave hunters looting his friends' graves.

"I know the human vultures will come," Tag's voice was low and intense. "But I will protect the ancient ones' home and whatever they left behind!" Even as he spoke the words, his mind questioned how.

Looking up into the cloudless sky, he whispered, "Great Taawa, God of the ancient ones, please help me find a way."

He adjusted the pack on his shoulders and eased himself, legs first, over the edge of the cliff. Tag searched with his feet for the first notch chiseled into the face of the cliff. *Where is it?* His heart pounded in his ears. His foot slipped into a toehold, and he lowered himself down, balancing in the notch while feeling for the next toehold with his other foot.

Tag rested his body against the face of the cliff. His fingers clung to mere cracks. He gazed down. The sheer wall below looked about a hundred feet high. Sweat poured into his eyes. "Don't look down!"

Tag aimed his eyes straight ahead at the multicolored limestone. He blinked to clear his eyes and took a deep breath. "Don't be such a wimp. Even if you do fall, it won't kill you." His halfhearted words died against the wall. He lowered his foot, feeling for the next notch. "Just break a leg or something," he mumbled, turning his head to the other side.

Two black bulging eyes glared back at him. A whiplike tongue lashed toward his face.

3

Tag jerked away from the bulging eyes and lashing tongue inches from his nose. His scream filled the canyon as his right foot slipped out of its toehold. He clung to the wall, feet flailing in the air. Sweat ran into his eyes. His nails broke. The wall became a blur as Tag plummeted downward.

I'm dead. . .

One foot—two feet, the skin on his cheek peeled off. Blasts of pain shot though his arms as they banged against the limestone. He slammed down into a heap at the base of the cliff.

Tag tasted blood and reached up to touch his mouth. His shaking hand missed his mouth and hit his cheek. A thousand pinpricks lit his face on fire. Through the sweat and tears, Tag saw blood on his hands. He fought off the wave of fear and pain sweeping his body.

He inspected his arms—scraped, banged up, but not broken. His legs were okay, but felt like Jell-O. Tag eased himself up. "You're all right," he reassured himself.

Tag looked up the cliff. What had he seen? The image of the hideous face filled his mind. *A lizard, a dumb old lizard!* Anger replaced his fear. *How could I have been so stupid, careless...lucky? What would have happened if I had broken my leg or gashed my head open?*

An unnatural silence pierced the sweltering air. He took a deep breath. Yes, he was lucky this time, but would his luck hold? Tag's scalp tightened.

The steep, narrow path leading to the village was unchanged except for the heat waves rolling off the boulders and deep ledges. Tag lived on the rim of the canyon with his parents for five years in the twentieth century, but he had never felt such heat in the canyon before. *It feels more like Phoenix in the summer than cool northern Arizona.* Tag wiped the sweat out of his eyes. Maybe he should have taken the shortcut up to the village. The thought of scaling up the forty-foot-high narrow chimney sent a shiver through him. No, the long way to the village was safer. It wasn't far now—just around the next bend.

Tag stopped short to catch his breath and steady his emotions. What would he find? What if there are still people living in the village? The speculation boomeranged through his mind, sending a sudden chill through his body. There could be. Hadn't he learned firsthand that anything was possible? Tag's heart hammered. Not everyone was going to follow Walker out of the canyon.

The sharp, angular face with thin lips pulled back in a snarl formed in Tag's mind. *Gray Wolf!* Fear flooded him. The politically ambitious nineteen-year-old native had accused them of being witches and had tried to kill Walker. Had Gray Wolf and his followers survived the sickness that forced Walker and the others to leave the canyon?

Tag's analytical mind scrambled for possibilities. Archaeologists believed the canyon was abandoned around A.D. 1250. Had Walker actually left with his people in 1250? Could it have been much earlier, say A.D. 1240 or even 1215? If it were earlier, then Gray Wolf could still be alive and in control.

Suddenly, he felt unsafe on the open path. Gray Wolf would kill him in a heartbeat. Tag slipped off the path and crouched beside a huge rock. Peering around at the walls of the canyon, he searched for signs of life. Should he take the risk and go to the village? It was safer, wiser just to go back to the cave and travel further into time. Tag tried to think through the panic that was taking over his mind and body.

"Of course, there isn't anyone left." The sound of his own voice took an edge of fear away. "I would have seen or heard someone by now." Tag stood up and started up the path again. His thundering heart was all he heard as he rounded the bend to the village.

Nestled under a cavelike overhang was a rock-and-mud wall. A low, T-shaped doorway stood in the center of the sturdy wall. Tag's heart felt as if it were going to explode. "Hello. Anyone home?" His words echoed off the wall in a hollow toll.

Memories swirled around Tag like a mist. "Let your heart see, as well as your eyes," the gentle words whispered out of the thick, low doorway.

"Singing Woman! This is your house." Tag touched the flat, limestone slabs neatly mortared with mud to form the front wall of the home. Warmth radiated from them. "Singing Woman." Tag closed his eyes. A round, reddish-brown face, a sea of wrinkles, appeared in his mind. Singing Woman's film-clouded eyes peered at him as if she were seeing him. She smiled and nodded as if to say, "Welcome."

Tag opened his eyes, moved to the door, and crouched down, his knees creaking. He placed his hands on the worn-smooth stone ledges at each side of the low doorway and crawled through.

A dry, acrid smell met his nose. The air was cooler inside. Tag stood just inside the door, waiting for his eyes to adjust to the semi-darkness. It was in this room that Walker had learned of his past. Tag tried to imagine what went through Walker's mind and heart when Singing Woman told him of his true heritage as an ancient one.

"All my life I have felt as if I have been on a tightrope balancing between the traditional ways of my people and the strange, demanding ways of the white man." Walker's words echoed in Tag's mind as his eyes came into focus.

You were, Walker. You were on a tightrope caught between times. Now, you are where you are meant to be, doing what you were sent to do. A lost feeling washed over Tag, leaving him feeling empty. *But where am I supposed to be? What am I supposed to do?*

"Be at peace my son, Taawa is with you," Great Owl's voice whispered through the abandoned home. "Let Taawa guide your steps."

Swallowing the tightness in his throat, Tag scanned the small room. The archaeologist inbred in him took hold, and he started taking mental notes.

The room was about eight by twelve feet. The limestone that formed the deep overhang also made up the back wall and ceiling. The front rock-and-mud wall met the low roof of the overhang to complete the dwelling. The ancient home remained a quiet testimonial to a good housekeeper.

Tag moved to the fire pit in the back corner. The woven

yucca mats covering the stone floor crackled under his shoes. Tag knelt next to the small cooking pit. A large brown ceramic cooking pot sat next to the burnt logs as if just taken off the fire. The pot was empty except for a thick layer of dust. Anything left in it would have been carried off long ago by rats or mice. Tag stood up and touched the low ceiling above the fire pit. Black soot smudged his fingers. Wiping his hands on his jeans, he studied the rest of the home. Singing Woman's neatly-organized ceramic dishes, storage baskets, sleeping mats, and a well-worn pair of yucca sandals waited patiently for their owner's return.

A shiver started at the base of Tag's spine. Had Singing Woman left with Walker? Could she have managed to climb out of the canyon? Being both old and blind would make the long journey to the Hopi mesas impossible for her. The shiver pulled at Tag's neck. Singing Woman had probably remained behind to die within the walls of her ancestral canyon. Tag's heart felt heavy. He would never know the fate of this kind and loving woman or all the other inhabitants of the village that would one day be known as the Sinagua Indians.

The gloom of depression invaded Singing Woman's home as Tag realized his dilemma. "I'm the one balancing on the tightrope now; walking time, belonging nowhere." His desperate words died in the silence of the mud-and-rock walls.

Tag hurried by more mud-and-rock cliff homes. There was no noticeable deterioration in the homes—in whatever time had past since he had left the ancient ones. Had it been a year, ten years, or fifty? Tag couldn't tell. Each thick, front wall was intact, standing strong against the harsh elements. Each home was silent, each T-shaped door empty except for memories swirling in and out, beckoning to him.

Just outside Littlest Star's home, a hand-held grinding-stone, a mano, lay on top of the boulder. Tag stopped next to the thigh-high metate. Its well-worn, rectangular grinding-trough was empty. Sadness tore at Tag's heart. In the future, thousands of tourists visiting Walnut Canyon National Monument, would pass this boulder. Many would stop to touch and speculate about this unusual metate. Yet not one would know the soft-spoken woman who had ingeniously used this boulder to grind corn on, hour after hour, day after day, so that her family would have corn cakes to eat.

Tag picked up the smooth, oval mano. Small flakes of corn lay hidden under it. *How long will these last in time?* Shaking his head, Tag replaced the mano. How long would the mano rest in its rightful place? *Until some thief steals it for his artifact collection or to use as a paperweight,* Tag's stomach churned at the thought.

At each house, faces and memories greeted Tag, enticing him into the past. The stark stillness of the canyon deepened his realization of being isolated in time.

Standing at the door of Great Owl's home, Tag felt over-whelmed. It was in this home that he had left most of him-self. He had lived here and grown to love the ancient ones. Sitting by Great Owl's fire he had learned that Walker was going to be the next High Chief. In this home, Tag had bid farewell to his little buddy, Small Cub. Had Small Cub escaped Masau'u's, the god of death, cold fingers? Or was his thin body buried somewhere nearby?

Something inside Tag urged him to enter, but dread kept his feet from moving. What would he find inside? What clues to Small Cub's fate lay within the T-shaped door? *Do I really want to know?* Tightness squeezed Tag's heart.

The smell of death and time met Tag's nose as he crawled through the low door. He strained to see. The room looked just the way he remembered last seeing it—or did it? The mat where Small Cub had lain sick was still next to the fire pit near the back of the room. A small brown ceramic drinking mug sat on the mat. Tag knelt. "Small Cub," he whispered, picking up the mug. Did this mean that Small Cub had died? Surely, he would have taken his treasured mug with him if he had lived.

Tag balanced the mug in one hand. Though small, the well-shaped ceramic mug was heavy. *No. It would have been just that much more weight to carry and could break. They would only take the bare necessities that were light to carry and not breakable.*

He was half-tempted to slip the mug into his backpack as a remembrance of Small Cub. No one would ever know. It was just a small, insignificant item.

"What is wrong with me?" Tag's firm words vibrated off the walls scolding him. He set the mug where he had found it. "It's just the same selfish thinking that pothunters have." Tag could almost hear his father's voice rather than his own bouncing off the walls. "What is wrong with you?"

Tag canvassed the rest of the house, neat as it had been when he first entered with Walker. Flute Maiden, Great Owl's daughter, had left it just as it was lived in; neat and organized. In the cooking area adjacent to the fire pit, tidy stacks of ceramic bowls, mugs, ladles, and pots stood waiting. Large ceramic food-storage jars with leather coverings stood next to the dishes. Tag knew without looking that they were empty. Every edible thing would be taken for the long journey.

"Most ceramic housewares were left behind." Tag took

19

mental inventory of the cooking area, "Except for the ceramic water jugs." Remembering hauling a full five-gallon jug up the canyon, he felt sorry for whoever carried them. How much water would Walker and his people find between here and the Hopi mesas? Worry nagged him.

Pivoting, he took the three or four steps to the opposite side of the room used for personal items. "The big baskets that stored their clothes are gone. Baskets would be the practical thing to haul belongings." He sounded like his dad again.

What else had been in this corner? The sleeping mats were still there, but the animal-skin blankets were missing. Yes, they had taken just the bare necessities. Tag shook his head. The ancient ones had lived with so little compared to the televisions, boom-boxes, microwaves, computers, and the countless other luxuries of the future.

Tag studied the home. Great Owl's family had left a lot that would reveal their lives to future generations: ceramic dishes, a small white basket decorated with a bold, black design, a wooden spindle, and a child's mug.

Memories of the past swirled around Tag. Small Cub's laughter and Flute Maiden's soft, musical voice floated in the warm air. He could feel White Badger's friendly presence and Great Owl's warm acceptance. Walker's smiling face rushed through Tag's mind, leaving his heart empty. Deadly silence filled the room. Time pressed down on Tag's shoulders like a huge yoke to be carried alone forever, without rest.

"What have I gotten myself into, and how am I going to get out?" Tag's desperate words died in the vastness of time.

4

T ag crawled out of Great Owl's home. The sun beat down into the canyon, casting oppressive shadows across its steep walls and ledges. Sweat trickled into his eyes.

I must be the only human being around for a hundred miles and five hundred years. Tag studied Great Owl's house and was glad that he came. His first stop in time had been productive, mentally cataloging what the ancient ones left behind. He had plenty to report to his dad.

If I ever make it back to him. The thought deepened Tag's loneliness. *At least everything is safe here for now. I'll just...*

The sound of shattering ceramic ware resonated through the stillness of the canyon. Somewhere close by, a deep, gravely voice called in a garble of fast-flowing words. A high, nasal voice responded with anger, followed by another crash of pottery. Tag's heart stopped. His ears strained to understand the alien words ringing through the sweltering air. The voices came closer. The hair on Tag's neck stood on end. It wasn't English or the ancient ones' language he heard.

Fear catapulted Tag. His feet stumbled over each other, and he landed with a thud just outside Great Owl's door. Before he could get up, a shrill, piercing third voice called somewhere to his left. The Gravel Voice answered up the path to the right.

I'm surrounded! Tag leaped up. The voices calling back and forth, were coming towards him. He scrambled through Great Owl's low doorway, smacking his head against the top of the doorway.

Stay calm, Tag's mind ordered his thundering heart. He crouched behind a large storage pot. The voices, muted through the four-foot-thick walls, called back and forth. They sounded like they were down the path from Great Owl's house. Who were they? From the sound of their language, they were Indian, but not modern day Hopi or Navajo, with which Tag was familiar. He pressed tighter against the pot. What were they doing here? Searching for food? Looting?

Times must be really tough if they are willing to get near the abandoned houses. He knew most Southwest Indian cultures traditionally avoided places of the dead for fear of evil spirits or witches.

Shrill Voice called right outside the door. *They're going to have a Powwow on Great Owl's doorstep.* Tag's heart rammed against his throat. *Think. There's got to be a way out. What would Walker do?*

Tag slithered across the room on his belly. Reaching the doorway, he peered out. A thin, dark-skinned man stood in the middle of the path. A good three inches shorter than Tag, he wore a scant loincloth. Loops of shells dangled from his

22

ears. A long, wooden bow hung from his left shoulder. Anger replaced Tag's fear. The small ceramic canteen suspended from the man's other shoulder belonged to Smallest Star! There was another crash of pottery. It sounded like it was one of the huge storage jars used for dried corn.

The man on the path screamed a shrill array of words. Tag pulled himself away from the door as Nasal Voice answered close by.

Okay, now what? It would only be a matter of minutes before one of them came in. What could he use to defend himself against three muscular men from another age? He looked around. Great Owl and White Badger had taken away all their bows, spears, and knives.

Knives! Tag reached for the small stone knife wedged in his waistband. Arrow Maker, the village stone-knapper, had given it to him. His hope faded as he clutched it. *It's sharp, but useless against three strong men. I have nothing else but the clothes on my back...*

"Things are dangerous here for strangers, and right now you'd look pretty strange to the ancient ones." Walker's once-spoken words whirled through Tag's mind, giving him an idea.

Tag slid away from the door and pulled off the canvas backpack. He fumbled it open, put the paho on the ground next to his leather loincloth, yanked out Walker's blue jeans, red Dodger T-shirt, and jogging shoes. *Nothing compared to hi-tech horror movie costumes in the future—hope these guys don't go to the movies a lot.* Walker's metal pencil-sized flashlight clanked to the ground. *Too bad it isn't dark, then I'd really scare the loin-cloths off them.* Tag shoved it back in the pack along with the paho.

23

Shrill Voice and Nasal Voice now prattled just outside the doorway. If only they would just stay out for a few more seconds, Tag thought. Gravel Voice joined them.

Just keep talking—have your high level executive meeting. Tag wrenched Walker's blue jeans onto his head. The legs dangled down over his shoulders like lop ears. He remembered Walker saying his clothes would come in handy sometime. Tag smiled. *How right you were, Walker.* He draped the loincloth over his own blue jeans. Tag tied Walker's shoelaces together. Slipping the pack onto his back, partially covering his hot-pink T-shirt, he chuckled. *A hump-backed witch!* But would it work? Fear knotted his stomach. *Great Taawa please, let these guys be superstitious.*

Tag crept to the doorway. The three men stood talking just a foot away. Nasal and Gravel Voice, dressed in garb similar to Shrill Voice's, were also short and thin, but muscular. Gravel Voice was proudly showing a small, decorated basket to the others.

That's Singing Woman's basket. Tag's anger burst into flame smothering his fear. He leaped out of the door. "You rotten thieves!"

The men swung around. Tag lunged at them. High over his head, he swung the jogging shoes like hunting bolos while waving the red shirt in his other hand. Pant legs flapped around his head. "Get out of here, you vultures!" Tag ran toward Gravel Voice whirling the shoes at him.

Gravel Voice's eyes grew huge staring up at the tall, hump-backed, blue-legged, pink-chested, speckle-faced, floppy-eared, big-footed spirit flying towards him. Dropping the basket, he jumped backward and toppled out of sight over the steep ledge.

Tag changed directions and charged the other two. They were already racing down the path. "Leave my friends' things alone you scavengers!" He chased them a few yards, howling and shrieking, with pant legs flapping, jogging shoes whirling, and Dodger shirt waving.

Nasal Voice looked over his shoulder. Tag hurled the shoes. They soared, twisting and turning like an uncoordinated bird, and hit Nasal Voice in the head. He screeched. Sprinting faster, he vanished around a sharp twist in the path.

Tag jerked to a stop. "Keep going you cowards! Don't come back or else I'll, I'll..."

What would he do? What could he do if the men suddenly found the courage to turn and face him? Tag spun around in a cloud of dust. A pant leg smacked him in the face. He tore back up the path in the opposite direction.

Tag jumped over pieces of broken pottery strewn in front of Littlest Star's house. Yucca floor mats and broken pottery littered the path in front of Arrow Maker's home nearby.

Tag hesitated at Singing Woman's house. He was seething. In just the few minutes since he had been there, her belongings had been looted. He wished he had picked up her basket where Gravel Voice dropped it. Now it would rot in the unrelenting Arizona elements.

"Every piece of pottery, each arrowhead, and bit of yucca cordage has a story to tell. When anyone steals or destroys even the smallest artifact, its story and the information learned from it disappears forever." His dad's regularly-given lecture blasted through Tag's mind.

"Dad, I couldn't stop them!" Tag cried. Sadness ripped at his heart as the need for breath tore at his lungs.

Tag flew over the hard-packed trail. He *had* to get back to the cave. Tears of frustration and anger blurred his eyes. He stumbled down. A pant leg lashed into his face with a sting. Tag whipped the jeans off his head as he barreled to his feet. In anger, he flung them in the air and hurled Walker's T-shirt after them. His feet pounded up the trail.

By the time Tag reached the cliff up to the cave, depression outweighed his anger. He scaled up the sheer wall. "I was a fool to even think I could pro..." He missed his footing but caught himself, "protect anything. It's impossible, simply impossible."

Holding the paho in his scraped and dirty hands, Tag felt emotionally and physically drained. "Why should I even try?" his voice reverberated within the cave. His stomach growled. His head and heart ached.

"Why should I even try, Great Owl?" Tag yelled. "Great Owl, I know you are watching!" Tears clouded his eyes. His knees felt weak. "Great Owl, please tell me what I am supposed to do. Please." The echo of Tag's pleading voice faded against the walls of the cave.

Tag looked down at the paho clenched in his fist and closed his eyes. He had no choice but to go on into time, with or without Great Owl's help.

Think good thoughts, positive thoughts. He leaned over the shrine with the paho. *Things have to get better. They can't get worse—or can they?*

5

T ag gently lifted the paho off the shrine the second time. His head pounded from time-walking and frustration. As he wrapped the paho in its buckskin, the memory of his first stop in time tormented him. How could he protect the canyon, its treasures and story against time and man?

With his head still throbbing in pain and uncertainty, Tag started down the cave's cliff. *Where am I in time now? How many years or centuries have I walked this time?*

He jumped down the last foot of the cliff and took a deep breath, trying to clear his foggy mind. Apprehension pulsated rhythmically with the pain in his head. What or whom must he face now?

The canyon had changed again. On the north side of the canyon, Tag saw a thick, green forest of pinion pines and junipers. Douglas fir trees covered the south rim of the canyon. Ponderosa pine and Gambel oak trees stood in thick groves on the west rim. The rocky ledges and shelves that had been barren, were now carpeted in sage brush, bee weed, wolf berry, cacti, blue grass, mutton grass, and other summer grasses.

"It looks more like the twentieth century than before," whispered Tag. Excitement doused his wariness. "But it doesn't smell or feel exactly right. Guess there is only one way to find out for sure." He trotted down the path toward the village.

The walls of Singing Woman's house looked almost the same as when he had last seen it. The limestone slabs were still in place forming a strong, thick wall. *Things look good so far.*

Tag crawled through the low, T-shaped doorway. Soft dirt seeped into his shoes. His eyes adjusted to the dim light as his nose singed with an acrid, dusty smell. Mounds of dirt, blown in over the years, blanketed the stone floor.

He hurried to the back of the room where the tops of the fire pit rocks peeked up through a bank of dirt. Tag couldn't see any of the cookware or dishes. "Whatever Deep Voice didn't destroy is probably buried under the dirt," Tag whispered. A strong urge to start digging swept over him. "No, things are safer buried, harder to find to steal."

Tag stopped and touched the smooth, empty trough of Littlest Star's metate. Her mano was nowhere in sight. Pottery sherds littered her doorway, but the walls were intact. Tag pushed on past the other homes.

Great Owl's and Morning Flower's adjoining houses stood strong and silent in the warmth of the sun. Relief pumped though Tag as he crawled through the low door.

His relief vanished. Recently, someone had dug in the drifts of dirt. Yucca floor mats protruded through the dirt where they had been pulled up. Flute Maiden's bowls and pots lay in neat piles as if someone was returning any moment to cart them off.

Tag knelt beside the rotting mat next to the fire pit and gently pulled it free from the dirt. His throat tightened as he saw the handle of Small Cub's mug poking up in the dirt. He carefully dug around the ceramic handle. *It's still in one piece!* Tag dumped the dirt out of the small brown mug and inspected it.

"That's mine, you thief!"

Tag whirled around. A husky body was silhouetted in the doorway. "Who said you could come in here?" The teenager was about the same height as Tag, but heavier. His shaggy, dirty black hair looked like it was cut with a knife. As he moved closer, his body odor made Tag's eyes water. "This is my territory." Crude features and a large mouth carved in meanness made up the square face.

"When did Congress pass that legislation?" Tag tried to sound tough. His knees shook.

The boy grabbed the neck of Tag's T-shirt and pulled him close. "Real smart, ain't you?" His breath gagged Tag.

"Smart enough to know to brush my teeth." A hard blow knocked Tag's breath out. He doubled over. The mug was wrenched out of his hand. Tag tried to protest but couldn't because of the pain.

"Horace, who you talkin' to in there?" A pimpled face peered through the low doorway.

"Just some skinny rat trying to steal our stuff."

The newcomer, with just his head showing through the narrow doorway, glared at Tag. "He looks more like some old dirty sheep with all that curly hair. Don't recognize him, do you?"

"Haven't really looked at him, Kern." Horace grabbed the seat of Tag's pants and hurled him toward the doorway.

Tag fell face first below Kern's pimply face. Kern reached down, got hold of Tag's shirt, and dragged him through the doorway. Horace helped from the rear. Tag landed with a dusty thump outside the ruin. He didn't even try to get up.

"Who are you?" Kern demanded. He was the same size and age as Horace, fifteen or sixteen, and wore the same kind of denim overall pants without a shirt. Worn, heavy leather shoes without stockings covered his feet. Uneven, dirty, yellowish hair hung around his small ears.

Horace crawled out of Great Owl's house. In the bright light, he looked even meaner. "Don't matter who he is or who he ain't. He's stealing our stuff." Horace held up Small Cub's mug.

Kern took the mug with dirty hands that hadn't yet grown into the rest of his body. "Looks like he's mighty fond of this sorry lookin' piece of trash, wouldn't you say?" He hurled the mug against the stone wall.

As it shattered, Tag exploded. He slammed into Kern headfirst. Horace seized him from behind. "Let go of me!" Tag struggled, but Horace held him tight.

"What's that there tote on your back? You got more of our things in there, ain't you?" Kern ripped Tag's backpack off. "Never seen a pouch like this. Then I never seen anyone wearin' a shirt like that before neither. Wearin' pink around here is dangerous, boy."

"Look at them funny shoes." Horace shook Tag. "Where you from, kid?"

"Where people act like human beings." A knee slammed into Tag's kidney.

Horace laughed. "A New Yorker, I bet."

Kern pulled out Tag's ceramic canteen from the pack. "This here might fetch a nickel." He set it down on the ground. A grin spread across his grimy face. "Now what's this wrapped up all nice and pretty in buckskin?"

Tag's heart stopped. *The paho—my key into time!*

6

Tag fought Horace's death grip. Horace growled, "Hold still, you skinny rat."

"He's mighty concerned about whatever is all wrapped up in this here buckskin." Kern smiled, showing his rotted brown teeth. He unwrapped the paho and held it up. "Well, look here, Horace. Strange lookin' thing with feathers and all. Looks mighty old, must be worth somethi..."

"What might you be doing going through another man's belongings, Kern Greely?" a voice with a heavy brogue asked from behind the three boys.

Horace swung around, his grip loosening. Tag yanked away and sprang at Kern. His shoulder smashed into Kern's chest, as he snatched the paho. Kern toppled. Tag, clutching the paho, sprawled out on top of him, near the edge of the steep path. Kern started shoving.

Tag rolled toward the ledge. Someone grabbed the back of his pants and yanked him upwards. Kern scrambled to his feet, seized Tag's canteen, and disappeared down the path.

Tag swung around, fists flying, expecting to see Horace's ugly face. Instead, he met two steel-blue eyes staring out from under bushy red eyebrows.

"No use in fighting me, young man." The red-haired, fair-skinned man, caught Tag's hands. His grip was firm, but the look in his eyes, kind. He was three or four inches taller than Tag and smelled of campfire smoke and dust. His dark, heavy cotton pants showed signs of hard wear. The long-sleeved, striped cotton shirt that he wore had a low-cut collar. "Those two hoodlums skeedaddled, and I won't hurt you."

Something in the man's firm but gentle voice reached through Tag's anger, fear, and loneliness. He stopped tussling. The man, in his early twenties, released him, smiled, and put out his hand. "I'm Sean O'Farrell."

Tag slipped the paho into his waistband and took the man's large, rough hand. "Tag Grotewald. Thanks for helping me."

"Those two are the devil's own. I feel sorry for anyone that tangles with them. Are you all right?"

Tag picked up the piece of buckskin laying next to his backpack. "Yeah." He shoved the paho and buckskin in the pack. He felt Sean's eyes on him.

"Tag, that's a strange name."

"It's short for Trumount Abraham Grotewald." Tag buckled up the pack. He wished the man would stop asking so many questions.

"Can't say I know your parents."

Tag slung his pack on his back and stood up. "I'm just passing through." His stomach growled.

"I'd say it's about time to eat a bit of lunch, by the looks of the sun. I'm just getting back from a week of surveying and have plenty of rations left up in my wagon." Starting up the path, he glanced over his shoulder. "Care to join me?"

Tag's empty stomach won over his cautioning mind. He followed Sean up the dirt path.

"More beans?" Sean asked. Tag nodded, his mouth full. Sean opened another can with his knife. "How long since you ate last?"

Tag shoveled the last of the first can of beans into his mouth. "A couple of hundred years is all." He took a bite of cold biscuit. It was coarse, but tasted delicious.

Sean leaned back against the pine tree perched on the rim of the canyon. He watched Tag start on the second can of beans. "I remember how hungry I got when I first came to America."

"From Ireland?"

"Yes. I was about your age, twelve."

"With your parents?"

Sean's eyes glazed over as he stared at the San Francisco Peaks to the northwest. The horse hitched to the nearby box wagon whinnied and stamped its feet. A bee buzzed in the still air. "I came alone. My folks died in Ireland and my baby sister and three brothers before them." Sean looked back at Tag. "It's not easy to be alone and a darn shame if you don't have to be. Families, that's what life is all about."

Tag swallowed the beans in his mouth, a lump growing in his throat. He didn't like the way the conversation was going. "You're a surveyor?"

"I came here in 1880 to do the final survey for the railroad. It only took me a week to know this was where I wanted to settle down." Sean moved his arm in a wide circle.

"This area has everything, thick forests and colorful deserts, huge mountains and deep canyons." Sean paused, gazing down into the canyon below. His sharp eyes softened. "You take this canyon and its ruins for example. There is a mystery here, a real life mystery. Why did all the people who built those cliff houses leave? What could have made them abandon their safe, warm homes?"

Tag studied Sean's face washed in shadows of melancholy. He saw tears in the man's blue eyes.

"The first time I went down in the canyon, I felt a strong kinship with those people." Sean's eyes met Tag's. "I think they were forced to leave because of sickness and death, just like I was forced to leave Ireland. I feel the sorrow and pain they felt burying their loved ones. I know the sadness and fear they felt leaving the only home they knew."

Tag fought the tears pricking the backs of his eyes. He looked away from Sean, staring at the can of beans in his hand. The ache in his throat wouldn't let him swallow the food in his mouth.

Sean's voice finally broke the silence. "Three years ago in 1882, when the line came into Flagstaff, I left the railroad. I set up my own surveying company and have been my own man since." He leaned back against the tree again. "Doing well, I might add."

"Flagstaff must be growing." Tag took another bite of biscuit.

Sean stretched out his long legs and crossed them. "The railroad has made Flagstaff a real boom town. The lumber and cattle business are growing fast. People are moving in every day, setting up a new business or homesteading." Sean leaned forward, "There is even talk about putting a rail line right up to the rim of the Grand Canyon. Can you imagine that? When that happens, we'll have more tourists than a dog has fleas."

"Yeah, and they will all want to come see Walnut Canyon and take home a souvenir that once belonged to the ancient ones." The words burst out before Tag could edit them. He met Sean's studying eyes. "Well, it's true, and there won't be anything left of the ancient ones' culture for people in the future to see or to study."

Sean rubbed his close-shaven chin. "You're right, son. Horace and Kern are prime examples of what you are saying. I saw their horses when I was passing by. That's why I stopped to see what mischief they were up to. They'd steal their own mother's corset if they thought it would fetch a penny."

"What's being done to protect the canyon?" Tag slammed down the empty bean can. "There has to be something done, and done right now so that archaeologists in the future can. . ." Tag stopped, seeing the look on Sean's face.

"Now you are a fine one to be talking, considering what I saw you stash in your satchel there."

"The rightful owner gave that to me. I didn't steal it!" Tag bolted to his feet. "Thanks for the food. I need to get going." He felt Sean's hand on his shoulder.

"There's no need to hurry off, son. I believe you and agree with you. More *does* need to be done to preserve this canyon's treasures. My blood boils every time I come here and see more destruction than the last time. I'm not the only one who feels that way either." Sean dropped his hand from Tag's shoulder. "There are others who care also, but not many people have the time or energy to keep an eye on the canyon. We're always looking for people and ideas to help." He bent down and starting cleaning up the empty bean cans. "In fact, tomorrow I am meeting with two men from the Smithsonian Institution in Washington, D. C. They are here to study what you call the ancient ones. We're hoping they might have some ideas on how to help protect the canyon and its artifacts."

Sean looked straight into Tag's eyes. "If you're not in too much of a hurry to get wherever you're going, maybe you'd like to meet these men. You have some ideas too, I bet. There is plenty of room at my place for you, if you don't mind sleeping on the floor."

Warning bells went off in Tag's mind. His clothes alone, the hot-pink T-shirt and high-top jogging shoes, made him stand out. People were sure to notice him and ask questions with no easy answers. What if something happened so he couldn't get back to the cave before the time window shut? Did the moon have to be full to illuminate the passageway of time, or would a quarter-moon do?

"There is much for you to do here and now," Great Owl's voice sang in the trees'song.

Tag's body shuddered from the cold shiver racing up his back.

"Son, are you all right?" Sean touched his arm. Tag flinched. "You don't have to stay if you don't want too."

Tag's confused and frightened thoughts screamed, *But what will happen to the canyon if I don't?*

7

I need to stop for supplies," Sean said. The box wagon bumped along the rutted, dirt road. The sound of hammers pounding drowned out Sean's words. The aroma of freshly-cut lumber mingled with the smell of horses and dust. Tag saw five new, wooden houses under construction in this block alone. Most of the wooden frame houses they passed appeared new. People waved at Sean and he greeted each by name in his loud brogue. Tag felt the people scrutinizing him, and his apprehension grew by the minute.

"There sure is a lot of building going on," Tag said as they passed two large buildings in different stages of construction.

Sean nodded as he waved to one of the carpenters. "It's the result of last year's fire. With all the wooden buildings and no water to fight it, the fire took out all of Old Town. Most people are rebuilding here."

"No water?"

"There is plenty of lumber and grazing land around Flagstaff, but no water to speak of." Sean tipped his bowler hat at four men gathered in front of another new building. "There is only one dependable natural spring in this area."

"What about Lake Mary? It's only seven miles away. The town should pump its water here."

Sean pushed his bowler back on his head and stared at Tag. "Now, I don't know of any Lake Mary around here."

"But I've fished in it a hundred..." Tag bit off his words realizing his mistake. *How stupid can I be? Lake Mary is—or will be, a man-made lake. It probably hasn't even been thought of, yet.* Why hadn't he paid more attention to Flagstaff history in Social Studies? He felt Sean's eyes still on him. Things could get very tricky. Tag looked the other way. He'd have to watch everything he said.

"We call this Railroad Avenue," Sean said, as if trying to ease the sudden tension between them. "The rail depot is another reason folks are rebuilding here." The railroad tracks ran along the south side of the wide street. Wooden frame buildings lined the opposite side of the rutted road, facing the tracks. Tag counted three general stores, ten saloons and gambling halls, one bakery, and numerous other businesses. Women in bonnets and long dresses, carrying parasols, strolled along the wooden sidewalks. Men wore denim pants, bright suspenders, vests, long-sleeved shirts, and a surprising variety of hats. Many men's faces bristled with mustaches, beards or both.

On a corner, a large, one-story, stone-cut building stood out from all the wooden frame structures. A sign over the door read *Brannen and Company*. People milled around on the wide, wooden walk in front of the store. Horses, hitched to metal posts on the west side, flicked their tails at the numerous flies. A variety of wagons and carriages stood behind the building.

Sean maneuvered his huge wagon next to a fancy looking carriage and tied the reins to the hand brake. "Brannen's is busy as usual." He climbed out of the wagon. "I'm glad my order should be ready. Coming?"

It felt like the wagon had jarred every tooth in his head loose, while the wooden seat had flattened his behind.

Anything is better than staying in this wagon any longer, Tag thought, as he jumped down.

Two railroad boxcars stood directly across the street. "The Atlantic and Pacific Railroad Station," Tag read the sign on the boxcars. "But the Santa Fe Railroad..." He stopped, seeing Sean's look. Tag groaned inside. *The Atlantic and Pacific must be the original railroad through Flagstaff. The Santa Fe will buy out the Atlantic and Pacific sometime in the future.*

Tag smiled and pointed to the boxcars. "The Santa Fe Railroad has stations like that in other towns. It's a great idea recycling boxcars."

"Re-what?" Sean's eyes squinted as if to see him clearly.

Tag's stomach knotted up. "Recycling—reusing something in a new or different way."

"Never heard of such a thing." Sean shook his head, turned and went into the store. Tag followed, biting his tongue.

Brannen's store looked like a set for a western movie. Everything a person could need, in 1885, was stacked on shelves that reached to the ceiling. Harnesses, lanterns, ropes, an assortment of tools, and other strange-looking objects hung from the open-beam ceiling.

A high counter ran the length of one side of the store. A large man with a dark, handlebar mustache stood behind a massive cash register just inside the door. "Been expecting you Mr. O'Farrell," he greeted. "Your order is ready. You're going to feed those gents from Washington mighty good, by the looks of things. They came in on the train this morning and are with Michael Riordan now."

"Good. I am sure Michael will feed them till tomorrow." Sean leaned on the counter. "Mr. Brannen, this is Tag, my new assistant."

Tag put his hand out to shake. Mr. Brannen, hands still on the counter, inspected him from head to foot. His eyes shot back to Sean, questioning. Uneasiness flooded Tag.

"We'll be needing a few extra cans of stew, beans, peaches, and throw in a couple more pounds of flour, sugar, and coffee in my order, please," Sean said. "Call us when it's ready. We'll browse around." He strolled towards the back of the store, while speaking to the numerous shoppers.

Tag followed through the jungle of shelves that accommodated shoes, hats, washtubs, door knobs, baskets, coffee grinders, pots, kettles, dishes, tents, blankets, brooms, and hundreds of other items. He touched an item here and there, not knowing what some of them were. *Wait till I tell Mom about this.* A wave of homesickness swept through him. His mom loved searching for bargains in the malls as much as his dad loved hunting for ancient artifacts in dusty old ruins.

Two plump women in large bonnets fingered colorful bolts of material near the center of the store. A small boy with short pants and dirty bare feet stood next to them. He sucked his thumb with noisy slurps. The three looked up and stared at Tag.

"The green cloth would complement your eyes, Mrs. Whipple." Sean tipped his hat and moved on.

Whispers followed Tag. "Do you know that strange boy with Mr. O'Farrell?"

"No. But he hasn't had a bath in years."

"What kind of mother would let her child leave the house wearing such peculiar and filthy clothing?"

"Must be an orphan."

Tag ducked behind a display shelf of long underwear and corsets. He felt his face burning. His heart rammed against his ribs. *If I ever get out of here, I'll never leave the canyon again.*

Feeling eyes burning a hole through his back, Tag whipped around. The barefooted boy stood a few feet away. In between sucks on his thumb, he asked, "Where are you from? Why are you wearing that funny, pink shirt?" Slurp. "Don't your ma ever make you comb your hair?" Slurp. "What you got in that bag on your back?"

Sean appeared behind the boy. "Master Whipple, how's that thumb tasting today?"

Tag marched back through the store, without looking to his left or right. He climbed into the seat of the wagon. People on the sidewalk gawked at him. The warm air buzzed with their whispered questions and remarks. Tag sat on the hard seat; shoulders squared, trying to appear calm and confident. But his face was on fire, his stomach did double flips.

What is keeping Sean? Is he in there telling everyone about me? Tag stiffened with fear. Was Sean sending for the cops— sheriff or whatever they had in these days—to arrest him for being a runaway or something? *I'd better get out of here.* He started to climb out of the wagon.

Sean came out of the store carrying a wooden box. "This

is the last of it." He slid the box next to the other boxes already loaded in the back of the wagon. "That should last us the week we'll be at the canyon." Sean climbed in next to Tag, untied the wagon reins and said to his horse, "Let's go home, O'Riley." The wagon jolted down the street.

"One thing I can't tolerate is busy-bodies. Every man has a right to his own privacy, as long as it doesn't hurt anyone else." Sean flicked the reins. O'Riley picked up speed.

Sean's house was comfortably tidy. The kitchen and bedroom were more than enough for one person. The parlor, as Sean called it, served as his office. There was a small barn behind the house and an outhouse a few hundred feet beyond. Tag noticed a large tin washtub hanging on the side of the barn.

"Would you have enough water to spare for a bath?" Tag set down the last box of supplies on the kitchen table.

Sean hung his hat on a hook near the back door. "That I would, and enough for you to wash your clothes, too. Go get the tub. I'll find you some clothes to wear." He grinned. "And a comb."

Tag didn't know which was more fun, trying to bathe in cold water with his knees scrunched almost up to his chin or using a scrubbing board to wash his clothes on. Combing his curly hair proved painful. "Six hundred years worth of snarls and rat nests," Tag mumbled while pulling the comb through his thick tangles. "Mom would die—just die if she saw my hair like this."

Sean's old denim pants were huge at the waist, three inches too long, but clean. Tag rolled a deep cuff in the legs. The long-sleeved blue cotton shirt was soft from usage.

"You look good in that shirt," Sean said, as Tag came

back into the house after hanging his clothes up on the line outside. "The shirt is a might more practical to work in, too. Ready for dinner?"

Later, with a full stomach, Tag crawled into the bedroll of thick quilts on the parlor floor. Exhausted, he had been barely able to finish the fried chicken and hash browns that Sean cooked. So tired that he hadn't even asked the hundreds of questions he wanted to about the men from Washington.

Who could they be? Tag burrowed down into the handsewn nest. Apprehension swirled around his questions.

Got to be careful—got to keep my mouth shut.

Sleep took his questions and worries into its warm darkness.

8

$\mathbf{T}$ag tossed and twisted. The bedroll's quilts knotted around him like a mummy wrap. His dreams played themselves out in unrelenting black and gray shadows of reality.

The rectangular limestone slabs of Great Owl's house were a pile of rubble cascading down the steep canyon side. Yet the low, narrow T-shaped door stood like a skeleton under the deep overhang. Dark gray smoke drifted out of the doorway in lazy curlicues. Tag heard echoing voices in the smoke as it floated towards him, surrounding him in a hazy whirl.

"I don't want to leave our home!" Small Cub's voice cried, turning the haze a bluish color. "I want to take my mug with me."

Dark blue smoke glided out of the doorway and strayed up the pathway. "You must choose whom you will follow; Gray Wolf or me..."

"Walker, Walker," Tag called. His throat burned and his

eyes watered from the thick smoke. He waved his hands trying to clear the air. "Wait Walker. I want to come with you!" He tripped over his feet, landing on his knees.

The hollow echo of Great Owl's voice drifted out of the doorway in a plume of white smoke. "Time for you to do that which you were sent to do."

"What am I suppose to do? Just tell me, Great Owl!" Tag crept toward the doorway.

"Now is the time...Now..."

Tag crawled into the doorway. Thick black smoke billowed into his face "Witch!" Gray Wolf's thin high voice wailed. "Kill the witch!"

Tag fell through the life-stealing smoke into Great Owl's house. The air was sharp, clean.

"What are you doing in my territory?" Horace's ugly face pressed up against Tag's nose, his breath worse than death.

Kern's crude face appeared next to Horace's. "Stealing our stuff." His oversized, dirt-encrusted hands reached towards Tag.

"No!" Tag scrambled back out the doorway into a thick black vapor. Rushing to his feet, he bumped into someone.

"Here from Washington to inspect the ruins."

"Dad?" Tag strained to see. His father's square face stared back at him. "Dad!"

"There is too much damage, too much destruction." He turned his back on Tag.

"But I tried to stop it. Wait Dad! I'll do better. Dad don't go!" Tag's feet felt cemented. His father's tall, thin shape faded away in the dark mist. "Please Dad. I'll do better!"

Tag fought the quilts binding his chest and arms and jerked straight up. "Dad I want to come home!" His own scream brought his eyes open. Tag's heart slammed against his chest. A lump in his throat blocked his air.

"Son, are you all right?" a thick Irish brogue called through the darkness.

Tag fought for breath. *Where am I?* Moonlight streamed through a small window above his head. Ghostly shapes loomed around him. Tag saw a flicker of light coming towards him. He gasped and tried to bolt to his feet. The quilts held him down.

"It's all right, son." Sean knelt beside him, holding a lantern. Its light cast dancing shadows around the room. "Tag, you were dreaming." He put his arm around Tag's shoulders. "Just a nightmare. Everything is going to be fine. You are safe here with me."

Tag fought to catch his breath. Everything was a blur of tears. He relaxed in the security of Sean's arms. "I just want to go home," Tag managed to say between sobs.

"I know son." Sean held him tighter. "And I'll help any way I can."

* * *

The sun's warmth filled the nippy early-morning air. Tag bumped up and down on the wooden seat in Sean's wagon. Despite the brightness of the morning, the memory of his nightmare still tormented him. Homesickness ate at his heart.

"I'd like to get camp set up before the others get to the canyon." Sean straightened his hat. "I thought the spot where we had lunch would be a good campsite." He looked over to Tag. "What do you think, son?"

"It is close to the trailhead; that makes it convenient."

Sean nodded. "That is a good thing to think about."

"Especially since I am the gofer."

"The what?"

Tag squirmed. His face felt hot. "*Gofer,* it's sort of a pun; I'll go-for this and go-for that."

Sean laughed and shook his head. "You come up with the most peculiar things." He started humming an Irish-sounding tune as he flicked O'Riley's reins.

Tag swallowed hard and turned to watch the scenery. He knew he was lucky that Sean didn't believe in prying. Sean hadn't questioned him this morning about his nightmare or the things he had said last night. He had fallen asleep with Sean sitting by his side. This morning, it was like it had never happened. Tag's stomach twisted. How long could he stay before Sean would start asking questions? *Not long if I keep saying such dumb things.* He'd have to walk a tight line.

A huge, blue-black raven circled overhead. The sun glinted off its long silky wings. Tag watched its effortless flight. It swirled down closer. Its harsh cry was a taunting laugh, "Caught, caught, Tag caught."

A two-seated, covered carriage and team of horses stood waiting near the trailhead at Walnut Canyon. Sean tied O'Riley near the carriage and mumbled, "I can never get a step ahead of Michael Riordan." He started down the trail at a brisk pace. Tag followed on his heels.

Rounding a bend, Tag saw two men standing in front of Singing Woman's house. They swung around.

"Morning, Sean," said the younger man in an eastern accent. Like Sean, he was clean-shaven and in his early twenties. Though he wore a broad-rim felt hat, high leather boots, and work clothes, his bearing was that of a doctor or lawyer. "I was wondering how long you were going to sleep in."

"Michael Riordan, only you would start out to the canyon when the moon was still a shining." Sean shook his hand. Turning to the older man he said, "James, it is good to see you again. I'm glad that you came back."

James Stevenson was a bit shorter than Sean and twenty years older. Graying, black hair showed under his broad-rimmed straw hat. He wore a neatly-trimmed mustache. "A year is too long," he nodded toward Singing Woman's house, "judging from the deterioration and destruction I've seen already. We are lucky the Major agreed to come. He wields a lot of power in Washington as the Federal Director of Survey and the new Director of the Bureau of Ethnology."

"A name that I hope to change to the Bureau of American Ethnology," a robust voice said from Singing Woman's doorway. A man with a black bowler hat, a long gray beard, and weathered skin crawled through the door. His denim pants were tucked into his high leather boots. He wore a dark vest and long-sleeved white shirt. The right arm of his shirt hung empty.

"Major John Wesley Powell!" Tag burst out. "I didn't know that you ever came to Walnut Canyon!"

Major Powell held out his left hand to Tag. His grip was iron. "It's my first trip here, but not my last."

"I've read both of your journals on your explorations down the Colorado River." Tag pumped Powell's hand. "They are fascinating."

Major Powell dropped Tag's hand. "Must have been one of my men's journals. Mine hasn't been published yet."

"Major Powell, I'm Sean O'Farrell." Sean took Major

Powell's hand. "I'm sure you'll find the ruins and relics here interesting."

"What little I have seen is most interesting." Major Powell stared at Tag.

"This is Tag," Sean put his arm around Tag's shoulder and moved him toward the other men. "Tag meet James Stevenson, an archaeologist from the Smithsonian Institution. And this is Michael Riordan, one of the towns-people interested in the ruins."

"Nice to meet you," Tag muttered. He felt Major Powell still scrutinizing him.

"Shall we get started, men?" Sean suggested. "Tag and I will go up to get the picks and shovels."

James Stevenson spoke up, "Let's wait on the tools. I want to show the Major more of the ruins before we decide where to excavate first." He started up the path with Michael Riordan close behind.

"Perhaps you know something about ancient cultures, young man?" Major Powell's eyes measured Tag.

Tag nodded.

"Good. We'll have plenty to talk about."

Tag wished he *could* talk.

9

Tag knelt elbow-to-elbow beside Major John Wesley Powell in Arrow Maker's house. Someone had knocked out the narrow T-shaped door, enlarging it by three feet. Now, bright morning light streamed through the gap. Tag carefully sifted through the loose, gritty dirt in the back of the house.

"Here is another piece of obsidian, a big one." Tag brushed the dirt off the black rock. "It has chip marks on it, too."

Major Powell took the fist-sized rock and studied it. "Smaller pieces have been chipped away from it, probably for arrowheads. It is strange that we have found so many little chips of obsidian in this ruin and now this larger piece."

Tag emptied the dirt from the trowel he held. "Maybe a stone knapper lived here."

"Interesting thought, but I doubt that a knapper would work *inside* a house since it is such cramped quarters." Major Powell slipped the obsidian into a wooden box with the other flakes of obsidian found in the same pile of dirt.

Tag pictured Arrow Maker in his mind; the friendly eyes, the steady hands, the long yellow cape covering the hump on his back, and the uneven legs that made walking difficult. Of course Arrow Maker stayed close to his home: it was easier for him. He remembered Arrow Maker always having a deer antler in his dark hands, chipping away at hunks of obsidian in the process of making arrowheads, knives, or spearheads.

"Maybe he took his work home at night," Tag suggested. He handed another obsidian chip to Major Powell. "He sat by the fire pit for light to work by."

"You think this was the fire pit?"

Tag met Major Powell's keen eyes. His hands suddenly felt sweaty. "Well, with the soot on the ceiling right above here, it seems logical."

"You are right." Major Powell smiled and went back to his digging. "You are very observant." He uncovered another good-sized rock. After dusting it off, he held it out to Tag. "What do you make of this?"

The eight- to ten-inch square rock was vesicular basalt. Tag ran his finger along the smooth groove running longitudinally through the center of the stone. "A shaft abrader." The words popped out of Tag's mouth before he thought. He clamped his mouth shut and stared down at the stone.

"Hmm, a shaft abrader *you think*," Major Powell peered at him. "Well, are you going to tell me how it was used?" He stroked his beard with his index finger and waited for Tag to answer.

Tag swallowed and squirmed around on his knees. "I...I..."

"Come boy. You are obviously very knowledgeable about Indian artifacts. Don't be shy. I want to hear your theory on how the *shaft abrader* was used."

"It's just a guess, but maybe the shaft of an arrow was put in the groove and rubbed back and forth to smooth and clean the shaft." Tag peered up at Major Powell. The man's eyes shot straight through him. "I'm probably totally wrong."

"But you aren't. Where did you learn so much about archaeology, boy?"

"Major Powell, have you found anything interesting?" Sean crawled through the doorway.

Major Powell stared at Tag. "Why yes, I think I have."

Tag jumped up. "Here Sean, you can take my place. I've got to go, haven't gone for hours."

"After you finish, son, go see if Mr. Stevenson or Mr. Riordan need anything from the wagon." Sean put his hand on Tag's shoulder. "I'll be here if you need help."

The rest of the morning Tag kept away from Major Powell. He found being with James Stevenson less intimidating. Stevenson reminded Tag of his own father, with his intense interest, precise observations, and willingness to share his knowledge with others. Tag fought to keep his firsthand information about the ancient ones to himself, as the group speculated on the life-style of hundreds of years ago.

"After seeing the huge pueblo villages north of here, I suspect these people left to go live there. As the old saying goes, they thought that the grass was greener there," said Michael Riordan. He sat down outside one of the ruins and leaned against the front wall. Tag handed him a canteen and listened.

"I don't think so, Michael," Stevenson said, wiping his forehead. He pointed to the sturdy mud-and-rock wall of the ruin. "There was too much time and energy expended building all these cliff homes for the people to just pick up and move to another location so close. Tree rings in the area suggest a major draught hundreds of years ago. My guess is that the draught forced these people out."

Visions of Small Cub laying on his mat, dying of dehydration from vomiting and diarrhea, flashed through Tag's mind. *A death swifter than lightning forced them to leave.* He bit his tongue and blinked his tear-blurred eyes.

"The larger storage pots we found here last year are gone," Stevenson stated with disgust in his voice. The sun hung directly overhead now. He stood in front of Great Owl's house with Sean and Michael. Flute Maiden's pottery, which Tag had saved from Kern and Horace, lay at Stevenson's feet in a wooden box.

Tag leaned against the front wall of Morning Flower's adjoining home. He stared at his friend's pottery waiting to be hauled up to the wagon. His throat tightened.

"You are right, James." Sean dusted the loose dirt off his pants legs. "As more people move into the area, more come and take whatever suits their fancy."

Stevenson put his hands on his hips. "Disgusting! These artifacts survived hundreds of years before the white man came. Now they are being destroyed in a matter of months."

"The question is what can be done to protect this area?" Major Powell asked, crawling out of Great Owl's doorway. He stood next to Sean.

Tag blurted out, "Laws need to be passed to protect antiquities." Everyone's eyes fell on him.

Major Powell looked at Stevenson and then at Tag. He stroked his beard in thought. "You might be right, son."

"I agree that *something* needs to done, but it will be pretty hard to enforce any such laws around here. Even cattle-thieving laws are near to impossible to uphold." Michael Riordan pointed to the pottery near his feet. "Not many people are willing or have the time to protect old pots."

"It has got to start sometime or there will be nothing left for future generations!" Tag took a step toward the men, his heart racing. "It's not just here, either. All over the Southwest there are thousand of ruins, big and small, being destroyed. The ancient ones' belongings and other artifacts are being stolen by the hundreds of thousands and along with them all the clues to the ancient ones' lives." Tag choked back the rest of what he wanted to say, realizing that he had already said too much.

"Laws," repeated Powell, gazing at Tag. "Laws."

Sean knelt down to the box of ceramic pots, bowls, and mugs. "James, are you planning on taking all of these back with you?"

"Yes, they are all excellent pieces." Stevenson squatted beside Sean. "Tag is correct about clues to the past. Why there is a wealth of information in this box alone." He held up Flute Maiden's large stew bowl. "This bowl is perfect for exhibiting at the Smithsonian."

Even though Stevenson was an archaeologist, Tag didn't want him to take any of his friend's things away, even to study. Flute Maiden's ceramic ware didn't belong back in Washington. The pieces belonged here where they were created, used, and loved.

Tears clouded Tag's eyes. He slipped into Morning Flower's doorway. He fought for control as his eyes focused in the dim light.

"Great Owl, what can I do?" Tag whispered. "What can I do? Great Owl, please tell me!"

Stillness echoed through the ruin.

If Great Owl was indeed watching, he was leaving things up to Tag to handle. "Great, just great!" Tag whispered and turned to leave. The numerous handprints in the mud plaster on the front wall caught his eye.

"They're still here!"

Tag slipped his hand into his own print, a print larger than the rest. He had made this print hundreds of years ago. The memory of the day he placed his hand in the wet mud plaster swirled around him.

Morning Flower's daughter had just been born, with Walker's help. The village women had come to replaster the walls. *It's our tradition to make our homes as fresh as possible after the birth of a child,* Tag heard Morning Flower's shy voice say as she cradled her hours-old daughter in her arms. Wrapped in a rabbit pelt blanket, the sleeping baby's mouth moved in a sucking motion.

"Tag," Sean's brogue startled Tag back into the present. Sean stood right behind him. Tag jerked his hand away from the wall.

Sean studied Tag's face. Silence and tension saturated the ruin. Finally, Sean said, "We're going down to the stand of walnut trees in the bottom of the canyon. Can you go get the box with our lunch and meet us there?"

"Sure." Tag hurried out the door.

Sean saw my hand in the print. Tag carried the box of food back down the path. The canvas pack bounced on his back as his worries jostled his mind. How much longer till Sean or the others demanded to know who he was?

Tag stopped in front of Littlest Star's house. He set the heavy wooden box down on her metate. He had to think things through before he saw Sean again. *It might be safer if I just left now. But how can I? There's so much to do right now that I can't...*

"Looks like we're just in time for lunch, Kern." Horace stood a few feet away from Tag. A mean smirk covered his grimy face.

"Yup. But first, we got us a skinny skunk to kill." Kern stood right behind Horace.

Tag bolted up the trail in the opposite direction.

"Get him!" hollered Kern.

Rocks slipped under Tag's shoes, almost bringing him down.

"Faster Horace."

Tag pushed harder. The trail became more overgrown with vegetation as it wound around a huge outcropping of limestone. Tag leaped over a rock, just missing a cactus. Rocks rolled. From behind, a scream of pain filled the air.

"Get up, Horace. He's getting away!"

"I can't. My ankle's twisted."

Tag kept running, but noticed a long, narrow crevice in the top of the rocks, some five feet above his head. Would it be deep enough for him to hide in? Could he even squeeze through the opening?

"Let me by, Horace. I'm going to get that stinkin' skunk."

Tag scaled upward on all fours. With his pack on, he couldn't squeeze into the narrow opening of the crevice. He slipped the pack off, pushed it in ahead of him. On his stomach, he wiggled into the crack. Rocks scraped his back and stomach as he slithered as far back into the crevice as he could. His lungs burned and his mouth felt like sandpaper. He tried to quiet his panting. Was he visible from the path?

He scrunched tighter against the back wall of the crevice. *Please, Great Taawa. Let Kern be nearsighted.*

Kern's foul words saturated the air below him. "He's disappeared—just vanished!"

"Help me, Kern. My ankle is swellin' up like a melon," Horace cried.

"You stupid fool, if you hadn't fallen we could've got him."

It seemed like hours till Kern's cussing and Horace's whining faded away. Tag wormed out of the crevice and climbed down. He looked around to get his bearings. The trail to the cave was above him. Kern was somewhere between him and the men in the bottom of the canyon. Could he make it down to Sean and the others without meeting up with Kern? Was being with the men an even greater risk?

Once or twice, Tag thought he heard something as he raced up the path to the cave. Each time he swung around, but he saw nothing and hurried on.

Sweat poured into his eyes as he scaled up the cliff. *Why doesn't this climb get easier?*

Tag heaved himself over the ledge and lay catching his breath. *I made it!*

He pulled up into a kneeling position. Opening the pack, Tag fumbled for the paho. Walker's flashlight rolled against his fingers. Tag hurried toward the cave's entrance. He felt the buckskin at the bottom of the pack. Tag pulled out the paho and began unwrapping it.

"Good thoughts, happy thoughts," he said.

Someone grabbed Tag's shoulder and jerked him around.

10

Kern's foul breath blasted Tag as his fist flew towards Tag's face.

Tag ducked and jammed an elbow into Kern's stomach. Sticking his foot in back of Kern's, he shoved. Kern fell backward in a cloud of dust. Tag raced through the cave's entrance.

Good thoughts, positive thoughts. Tag lunged toward the shrine with the outstretched paho. *Please Taawa, don't let Kern come with me!*

The cave exploded with thunder.

* * *

Air finally found its way into Tag's lungs. He took gulping breaths. Pain hammered his head with each breath, and his thought processes began working again.

"Kern!" Tag forced his eyes open. His own shrill voice

pierced back through his head as it bounced off the cave's wall. He jerked up.

The cave was empty.

"Thank you," Tag whispered. "It doesn't matter *where* I am in time, as long as Kern's not with me."

The air in the cave was warm. It felt like late July or early August. Tag stretched out his cramped legs. His back creaked. He felt centuries old. "I guess I am," Tag said, getting up.

"I am...I am..." his words echoed around him.

Tag wrapped the paho up in its leather again. He opened the pack and placed it inside. "It could be 1993."

"19..." His echoed abruptly died.

Tag felt his scalp tighten, "But something tells me it's not."

"Not...not...not..."

Tramping out of the cave, he started climbing down the cliff as the echo resounded within the walls of the ancient cave.

"No!" Tag's words bounced off the canyon walls and back into his face as he stared at the pile of rubble that was once Singing Woman's house.

As soon as he had hiked down the main trail, Tag realized things had deteriorated. He had virtually followed a path of graffiti, rusty tin cans, beer bottles, and litter to Singing Woman's home, but he wasn't prepared for the destruction before him.

He scrambled over the pile of limestone slabs. Nothing remained of Singing Woman's belongings except numerous pottery sherds strewn all over the ground. Tin cans and broken glass bottles circled the fire pit, and half-burnt logs spoke of recent fires. Names and dates scrawled in glaring black paint, or carved deep into the limestone, covered the back wall and the low roof.

Tag pivoted, surveying the destruction, still not accepting it. His knees shook and his empty stomach twisted in fury. "They didn't listen. No one did a blasted thing to help!"

Rectangular rock slabs shot out from under his shoes as he climbed out of the rubble of Singing Woman's home. Many of the bricklike slabs littered the steep side of the ledge in front of the ruin. *How did they get so far down the hill?*

Tag's surface emotions, the anger and frustration, urged him to go back to the cave. *It's useless. You can't change history.* Yet the archaeologist, deep within him, demanded that he see the full extent of the damage. Homesickness welled up in his chest. He wished he could crawl into his dad's strong, capable arms.

"There is something for you to do here," Great Owl's voice whispered amidst the devastation.

The hair on Tag's neck stood up. He wiped his teary eyes with the back of his hand. "But what?" His question blew away in the breeze.

The next group of ruins looked better. The long, continuous walls that made up five homes stood intact, although the T-shaped doorways were no longer recognizable. Tag crawled over the debris and through the gap where the first doorway had once stood. Decay singed his nose. Large pieces of yucca mats lay in a pile with pottery sherds and tin cans. Small brown corncobs lay in a heap in one corner. A once-neat pile of yucca cordage used for rabbit snares lay scattered nearby. *Whose house was this?* Tag searched his memory. *Scar Cheek's or Fawn's?*

Tag started to climb out through the irregular opening.

He spied something wedged in between the rock slabs. *What?* Tag picked it up. *A dynamite fuse! Someone blew the doorway out to have more light to pothunt!* His anger exploded. Walls that took hours of tedious and strenuous work to build had been blown apart in seconds by greed. He stared at the steep ledge below the house and realized why the stone slabs from the wall now littered the hillside.

"How can man be so stupid?" Tag screamed. He hurled a broken slab as far as he could over the edge of the path.

Tag touched the smooth, empty trough of Littlest Star's metate, surprised that someone hadn't blown it apart, too. The front wall of Littlest Star's house still remained intact. Hope swelled in Tag's heart. *Maybe Great Owls' home is okay too!*

The destruction was random. Many of the walls had gapping holes, while others stood strong and whole. Tin cans, bottles, and yellowing newspaper littered the doorways. Tag knew he should stop and get a date off one of the brittle newspapers, but the uncertainty of the state of Great Owl's home spurred him on.

"Yes!" Both Great Owl's and Morning Flower's adjoining home showed no significant damage. Crawling inside Great Owl's house, Tag saw that it was cleaned out right down to the bare limestone floor. Not even a pottery sherd remained.

"These two ruins were excavated some thirty years ago, back in 1885, by Richard Stevenson." The gravely voice, coming from just outside the doorway startled Tag. "Everything found in these ruins is on display at the Smithsonian Institution back in Washington D. C." The voice had a definite New York accent. "Everything that is, but the handprints in the mud plaster. You can see these ancient prints best in the ruin on the right. Go ahead and go on in. Watch your head, please."

It would be only a matter of seconds before someone came into Great Owl's house. Tag pressed himself against the corner of the front wall.

A child's voice screeched, "The ghost boy!"

"Don't be ridiculous, dear." A large, flowered bonnet poked through the T-shaped doorway. "That's only a story— *ahhh!*" The woman's head disappeared.

A man's head and shoulders reappeared. "Come out here, boy," his gravely voice ordered.

Tag gulped down his heart and crawled out. An elderly man, a middle-aged woman, and two small children hiding behind the woman's long full skirts, stood on the path.

"What are you doing in there?" Deep lines molded the long face of the man, in his late sixties. He wore denim pants, a long-sleeved shirt, high black boots, and a sagging felt hat.

Tag tried to sound innocent. "Looking around like everyone else."

"Don't remember you coming out with this group." The man stared over his wire-rimmed eyeglasses at Tag.

"He's not with us, Mr. Pierce," stated the woman. She folded her arms across her ample chest, "And I certainly don't want him with us. Heaven only knows where he came from and *what* he brought with him." She swung around almost knocking down the little girl still hiding behind her skirt. "Come children. Let's go on."

Mr. Pierce pondered Tag. "How did you get out here, boy?"

"Walked."

"Good long jaunt from town," Mr. Pierce rubbed his stubby chin. "Been here before?"

"A couple of times. My dad was...is, an archaeologist. The ruins are great, aren't they? Sort of like walking back into time and all." Tag moved. "Well, I got to be going."

Mr. Pierce blocked his path, "You must be mighty interested in dead Indians to come clear out here from town alone. Maybe, I can persuade Mrs. Ayer to let you ride back with them."

"No thanks." Tag nonchalantly dusted the dirt from the front of Sean's shirt. "I want to spend more time in the canyon, you know, just looking around."

"What's your name?"

"Tag."

Mr. Pierce inspected him up and down. "You're mighty skinny. Been a while since you ate?"

"Years."

"You go on up to the ranger cabin, and tell Mrs. Pierce to feed you. I'll be up after Mrs. Ayer and her children have seen enough. You need a place to sleep, too? Our front porch is a lot safer than sleeping out in the open with the bears." He moved to one side.

Tag hurried passed him. "Thanks, Mr. Pierce. I'll be happy to work for food and a place to sleep."

"Just you mind your manners around Mrs. Pierce. She's a bit persnickety about all the pleases and thank yous."

Tag trotted up the path. As soon as Mr. Pierce was out of sight, his first thought was to escape. He darted in the direction of the cave. His stomach growled in an angry response to his flight. "Quiet!" Tag put his hand on his empty stomach as he ran along. "I'll feed you at the next stop in..."

A cold breeze lashed Tag's face. He jerked to a stop. Tingling sensations ran up and down his spine.

"My son..."

"I know—I know!" Tag interrupted Great Owl's voice in the sudden cold breeze. "There is something I need to do here." He shrugged his shoulders, took a deep breath, and started back down the path. "I just wish you'd give me a little more help here, like telling me what it is I am supposed to do!"

11

Tag knew he could find the ranger cabin. It wasn't far from where the Visitor Center would stand in the nineteen-nineties. In the future, special ranger-guided tours would take a limited number of tourists to the old cabin, but he had walked there many times from his parents' trailer. It was one of his favorite getaway-to-be-alone places. What would it be like now, in 1916? His stomach twisted and growled in hunger. He sure hoped Mrs. Pierce was a good cook.

As Tag passed the destruction of Singing Woman's home, new determination thundered through him.

"I'll make them listen this time!" he vowed.

The wind whispered in the trees, "How?"

* * *

"Thank you, Mrs. Pierce," Tag took the tin plate heaped with scrambled eggs and thick slices of homemade wheat bread. His mouth watered at the aroma. "Thanks for letting me clean up also."

"You are more than welcome. Sit there on the front porch and eat," Mrs. Pierce said in a thick southern accent.

"Yes Ma'am. It looks delicious."

Mrs. Pierce was a good number of years younger than her husband. Her long dark hair was twisted in a tight knot on the top of her head. Her clear blue eyes inspected Tag openly. "It's just eggs. What did William think I would feed you at this time of day? That man is always sending hungry stomachs my way. Guess he remembers his own blue belly being empty all through the War Between the States."

Shoveling in the eggs, Tag nodded.

"You're pretty young to be out on your own. What are you? Fifteen or sixteen? But then, fifteen was plenty old for our southern boys to put on the gray and die." She reached back and adjusted the strings to the white apron covering her long, calico dress. "My daddy was but eighteen when he fought at Antietam. He lost both of his younger brothers in that battle. Well, eat up, and if you want more, just holler." The screen door slammed behind her.

What would she do, if she knew I was only twelve? Tag started in on the crusty bread. *It pays to be tall after all.*

Tag studied the log cabin as he ate. It wasn't very big, maybe two rooms. He knew that eventually additions would be added making it four rooms. A large garden grew on the east side of the cabin. An unhitched buckboard wagon stood by the corral in the back, while three horses rested in the shade of ponderosa pine trees at one end of it. Another horse, hitched to a two-seated, open carriage, waited patiently near the corral. An outhouse peeked through the scrub oak and pine trees beyond.

Tag tried to remember how long the cabin served as the

first ranger station. *Wasn't it 1930 or 40 something?* He looked toward the rim of the canyon to where the Park Service Visitor Center would be someday. *Will there be anything left for people to visit by then?*

Uneasiness snaked through Tag remembering Great Owl's words as they parted hundreds of years ago. "There is much your people must learn from the mistakes of my people. If your people are going to survive, they too must learn to live in peace and harmony with each other and with Mother Earth."

Frustration piped through Tag. *But no one listens to a skinny kid from nowhere!*

He heard the Ayer children's laughter. They appeared through the trees chasing each other. Mr. Pierce and Mrs. Ayer strolled behind. Mrs. Ayer stopped short when she saw Tag on the steps. "Henry and Gretchen, get into the carriage. Thank you, Mr. Pierce." She glared at Tag, shook her head, marched over to the carriage, and heaved herself up. "Please tell Mrs. Pierce good-bye for me."

The children stared at Tag as the carriage rolled by. "See, I told you. Ghosts do too eat," said the boy, pointing at Tag.

"Seems you have become the legendary ghost boy." Mr. Pierce eased himself down next to Tag and chuckled.

Tag set the empty plate down. "Ghost boy?"

"Story has it that some thirty years ago, local ruffians were digging in the ruins when a tall, thin, curly-headed boy appeared out of nowhere. The mysterious boy beat up the ruffians, broke one of their ankles, and then just disappeared into thin air with a huge clap of thunder. That nasty break caused poor old Horace to limp ever since." Mr. Pierce took off his hat and drew out a red bandanna from his pocket. "Many people claim to have seen the ghost boy drifting in and out of the ruins just after dusk." He wiped his high forehead. "Some say he's searching for his family who abandoned him here, but others say he's the guardian spirit of the canyon sent by some Indian deity."

"People really believe that?"

"Yup." Mr. Pierce smiled and put his bandanna back in his pocket. "Course, I don't refute it none. The stories tend to keep people out of my hair after sunset, especially Horace."

The sound of wagon wheels and voices drifted through the trees. "Another group is coming, and I haven't even rested up yet. More and more people come each summer. We had right near four hundred last year alone. Why, some people are even driving horseless carriages clear out here." Mr. Pierce shook his head. "I don't know why any man would want such a loud, smelly contraption. Now you take those black Tin Lizzies made by that New Yorker, Henry Ford. Everyone is buying them, but with gasoline costing a whole quarter a gallon it is too expensive for anyone to fill up the tank! Good thing too, because when you go up a steep hill, likely as not, the gas tank under the front seat slops all over your boots. That's not my idea of progress. No sir. Just give me a good team of horses and a sturdy wagon any day."

A buckboard, driven by a large man, appeared between the tall pines on the dirt road. Two women sat beside him. A variety of people filled the back of the wagon.

"Quite a group," Mr. Pierce said, standing up. "Automobiles will never replace the good old wagon for groups that big."

"I'll take my plate inside to Mrs. Pierce, and see if there is anything she needs done." Tag had no desire to meet the newcomers. He tapped on the screen door and went in.

A small, horsehair settee, an oak rocking chair, and a desk stacked with papers occupied the front of the room. Red and black Navajo rugs covered much of the pine-plank floor. A long shelf displaying the ancient ones' pottery and baskets ran along the front wall. Tag's stomach knotted up. He tore his eyes away from the shelf that flaunted his ancient friends' personal belongings.

An oak table with an oilcloth covering and two pressed-back oak chairs stood near the rear of the room by a large iron cookstove and a dry sink. He could see a narrow, quilt-covered bed in the room off to the left.

"Thank you. It is the best meal that I've had in years." Tag set the plate on the dry sink. "Can I help you with anything, Mrs. Pierce?"

"Know how to weed?" Mrs. Pierce answered without looking up from the pot she was stirring.

Tag went out the back door and toward the garden, keeping his head down. He knelt between the tall stalks of corn, keeping his back toward the corral where the people piled out of the wagon.

"Right nice day for a picnic," Mr. Pierce's voice said. "I just got back from taking another group down, so I'm a bit tired."

"Don't worry, Mr. Pierce, we know the way," answered a husky voice. "We'll do just fine on our own."

Tag peeked through the stalks. There were at least eight people carrying huge picnic baskets on their arms.

"I'm sure you will. I'll walk down in a bit and just remind everyone they are not allowed to dig in the ruins for artifacts. What's lying around in sight is one thing, but digging for mementos is another."

Tag bit his tongue as he watched Mr. Pierce lead the group toward the trailhead. He yanked out a weed and threw it over his shoulder. *Eight picnic baskets! I bet Mr. Pierce won't even search the baskets when those vultures come back.* Tag pitched another weed over his head.

"I was right," Tag whispered hours later. He stood behind the screen door of the cabin watching the picnickers hoisting their heavy baskets into the wagon. "He's not even going to *ask* if they took anything." Desperation replaced his anger. What could he do?

"You must be hungry," Mrs. Pierce came through the door, "after all the weeding and wood-cutting you did this afternoon. Dinner will be ready soon. Go on out and sit with Mr. Pierce till it's ready."

How can I explain it all to him? Tag thought, watching Mr. Pierce whittling a toothpick from a twig. How does someone tell an old man, who fought in the Civil War, to get tough and do the job that he was hired to do?

"Mrs. Pierce said you did a good job on the garden and filled the woodbox too." Mr. Pierce snapped his pocket knife shut. "She's cooking chicken and dumplings tonight." He inspected the toothpick and slipped it into his shirt pocket. "We'll get a bedroll made up here on the porch before it gets dark. Glad you're spending the night."

"I appreciate you inviting me." Tag said, looking out into the forest. *It's useless. Even if I knew how to say it, Mr. Pierce wouldn't change. He's just too kindhearted.* His anger died. The weariness that depression brings flooded over him.

I'm fighting a no-win battle against time and man.

12

Tag pushed his plate away. "Mrs. Pierce, that was the best breakfast I have had in at least thirty years. Thank you."

"Thirty years, you don't say." Mrs. Pierce chuckled, dismissing Tag's truthfulness as a joke. "I'd have guessed at least fifty years by the looks of those ribs sticking through your skinny chest."

Mr. Pierce stood up from the table. "You stay with us a while and Mrs. Pierce will fatten you up good. She's the best cook in the North, South, and Southwest." He winked at his wife as she cleared the table. "Well, Tag, do you think you could help with special folks visiting the canyon today?" He strolled toward the front door.

"Sure!" Tag rushed to hold the door open. "You just tell me where you want me to take them."

Mr. Pierce peered over his round wire-rimmed glasses. "It sounds like you're trying to steal my job from me."

"Oh, no sir. I just want to..." Tag's face felt hot.

Mr. Pierce eased himself down on the porch step. He winked at Tag. "I'm just funning with you. Although, it might be best for you to come along with me a few times to learn the ins-and-outs of the rangering before you start out on your own."

"Yes, sir. Whatever you say. I don't know as much as you do about the canyon, but I want to learn."

Mr. Pierce dug into his back pants pocket and pulled out his bandanna. "Word came yesterday that the Coltons would be back today."

"The Coltons?" Tag tried to keep his excitement out of his voice.

"Dr. Harold and Mary-Russell Colton from Pennsylvania. Do you know them? No? I didn't think that you did." Mr. Pierce took off his glasses. "Dr. Colton is a professor at the University of Pennsylvania. Studies animals, I believe. His wife is a well-known artist." Mr. Pierce spit on his glasses and wiped them in careful strokes with his bandanna. "They came to the canyon four years ago on their honeymoon. They've been back every summer since. Seems they enjoy our little display of ancient life here. Might as well move here, I say. But then they are northerners, and northerners are not the brightest at times." Mr. Pierce plopped his glasses back on his thin nose. "But don't tell Mrs. Pierce I said that."

Tag nodded, trying to keep from doing an Irish jig right there. He knew the Coltons, not personally, of course. They died before he was born, but he knew of them. Dr. Harold Sellers Colton and Mary-Russell Colton established the Museum of Northern Arizona and dedicated it to the preservation and study of ancient and contemporary Indian cultures. It was one of the few places that both he and his dad loved. His dad didn't care for sports, movies, TV, or even video arcades, all the things Tag loved. Archaeology seemed to consume his dad twenty-four hours a day. Homesickness welled up in Tag's heart, remembering the hours spent with him at the museum. Because of his dad's job with the Park Service, together they were allowed to explore a huge, private storage room with ceiling-high shelves. Each gray metal shelf held hundreds of artifacts—from pottery to stone tools and shell jewelry. Dad took hours explaining different items on the high shelves; how they were made and used, and where they came from. Tag especially enjoyed all the interesting or strange tidbits of information Dad added. It was during these hours that Tag had truly felt close to his father. He had gained most of his archaeology knowledge at his dad's elbow while exploring the Museum of Northern Arizona.

Now, Tag's eyes stung with little bullets of tears. *Please Taawa. Let me go there again with Dad,* Tag prayed as a dusty black automobile bounced up the road to the cabin.

*   *   *

"Mr. Pierce said that you are from Pennsylvania. Aren't the winters awfully cold there?" Tag asked as he and Dr. Colton stood outside Great Owl's home. Mrs. Colton and their two-year-old son, Ferrell, were exploring some of the other ruins.

"Yes, and they seem to get colder each year." Dr. Colton had a long face with a beard and mustache. Dressed in work clothes, he reminded Tag of his dad's archaeologist friends in the future. Dr. Colton's intense eyes missed nothing as he crawled in and out of the ruins. "I've never been here in the winter, but it must be beautiful with the snow on the San Francisco Peaks."

"The Peaks are gorgeous and have great skiing, too."

Dr. Colton peered at Tag. "Skiing?"

Realizing his time-error, Tag rushed on. "And then there is the Grand Canyon, it's just a few hours away. You haven't lived until you have seen the Grand Canyon in the winter. It is perfect for Mrs. Colton to paint, and there are all kinds of wild animals for you to study. I'm sure that the University in Flagstaff needs a good zoology professor."

"University? Do you mean the Normal School?" Dr. Colton rubbed his beard. "It's only a few years old. I'm not sure if the school even has a zoology department."

"You are the perfect person to start it. Of course, you'll need a *museum* to display all the fossils and dinosaurs you'll find. You know that northern Arizona doesn't have a museum at all, which is a real shame considering all the Indian ruins and artifacts around. And..."

Dr. Colton held his hands up, "Wait a minute, young man. Do your parents have land to sell, or has Flagstaff hired you to promote their town?"

"No, it's nothing like that." Tag shifted uncomfortably and ran his fingers through his hair, getting them tangled in his tight curls. "I—I just love Flagstaff so much that I think everyone should move here, especially someone like you."

"You sound just like Sean O'Farrell." Dr. Colton started down the path away from Great Owl's house.

Tag's heart stopped. "You knew—know Sean?" He ran after Dr. Colton. Could Sean still be alive?

"We had dinner with him at his house last night, along with his wife, Kathryn, and their youngest son, Michael T. If

74

I remember correctly, Sean was the one that advised us to come to Walnut Canyon first."

"Papa!" Colton's own son, Ferrell, called. His dark hair twisted and curled with sweat, despite the short, blue, dress-like outfit he wore. His small, black boots came to above his ankles and laced up the front. He scurried up the narrow path on chubby bare legs with Mrs. Colton close behind. "Papa, look." He held his tiny hand up to his father.

Dr. Colton knelt and put his arm around Ferrell. "Let's see what great treasure you've found."

Ferrell opened his fist and held out a piece of broken pottery about the size of a half-dollar.

"Well, well." Dr. Colton turned the sherd over in his hand. "This is a treasure. The black design on the white pottery is striking. I didn't realize that these Indians painted their pottery."

Tag couldn't resist. "They didn't."

"Oh?" Mrs. Colton said, joining the group. She was a petite woman with pleasant blue eyes. Her long, split skirt made climbing into the ruins easier. "Mr. Pierce said many of the pottery sherds around have designs on them."

"He's right. The ancient ones who lived here didn't paint their own pottery, though. They traded for it." Tag saw Mr. Pierce working his way up the path. "I'm sure Mr. Pierce can tell you more about it."

"More, more rocks," Ferrell bounced up and down clutching his father's pant legs.

Dr. Colton picked him up and squeezed him. "Maybe Tag can help you find more sherds."

"Is everything all right with you folks?" Mr. Pierce said, stopping next to Mrs. Colton. "Sorry I had to leave you all, but I had another group of visitors that I needed to check on."

"We are fine, William. Tag was just explaining how the painted pottery was not made here, but was bartered for." Dr. Colton handed the sherd to his wife. "Fascinating isn't it, Mary? Such a distinctive design."

"I wonder if each tribe or geographic area created and used its own paint colors and specific designs?" Mrs. Colton examined the sherd with her long fingers. "If they did, then you could determine where each piece of ceramic was made."

Dr. Colton added with interest, "That information also gives clues to trade routes. William, did the different geographic groups have their own pottery designs?"

Mr. Pierce rubbed his chin and gazed at Tag. "That's a good question."

"Ferrell, let's go look for some more sherds." Tag said trying not to sound too eager to escape Mr. Pierce's penetrating stare.

"More pretty rocks," Ferrell stated, half an hour later. He squatted in the middle of the path. He dropped the three small sherds in his chubby hand to pick up a large, black-on-red sherd near his feet.

"Sherds, Ferrell. They are sherds." Tag knelt next to the child. This was the fourteenth time Ferrell had stopped to exchange the sherds he clutched. "You can't carry them all, so which one do you want to take?" Tag smiled watching the toddler playing with the sherds at his feet. *He's so cute. I wonder if all two-year-olds are like Ferrell?*

The memory of another young boy, Small Cub, took over Tag's mind. Despite the language barrier between them, he remembered talking to Small Cub just like he did to Ferrell.

Small Cub was a chatterbox too. Though he tried, Tag couldn't picture Small Cub even being any other age than four. Where was Small Cub now? Goose bumps covered Tag's arms at the thought, and he pushed the obvious answer out of his mind.

Tag held his arms out for Ferrell. "Come on, big guy. We'd better go find your parents."

Two men appeared on the trail above. Each hauled a huge picnic hamper. "The black and white pot alone is worth a dollar." The taller man's huge nose looked like a hooked beak.

The second man, in a bright red shirt, with a bald head reminded Tag of a turkey vulture. "Not bad for just an hour's work. The little bowls I dug up are worth a nickel each." The two stopped chatting when they saw Tag and Ferrell.

Tag stood up and stared at the men as they moved closer. Which one of his friends' belongings were stashed in the men's picnic baskets: Littlest Star's stew bowls or maybe one of Fawn's beautifully-shaped vases? Anger consumed Tag. He cleared his throat. "Nice day, isn't it?" He figured starting out friendly was safer.

"Right nice," Turkey Vulture said. His eyes were small, sunken, black slits.

Tag stood in the middle of the path blocking the men. "I think it is best for me to warn you that it is against the law to steal anything from the ruins." He tried to make his voice deep.

Beak Nose glared. "You don't say. Now move aside."

"Those baskets look heavy." Tag's knees began to shake. How far did he dare push, especially with Ferrell to worry about?

"What's in our baskets is none of your concern," anger rimmed Turkey Vulture's voice. "Move aside." With a hard shove he knocked Tag to one side and scrambled around Ferrell, still squatting in the path.

"Best keep your mouth shut, boy." Beak Nose threatened as he jostled past Tag. With long strides he followed his companion around a bend in the path.

"Well, here they are," Mr. Pierce's voice said, behind Tag. "Looks like the boys have had a right good time together."

Ferrell rushed toward his mother and father. "Look, pretty rocks."

Tag clenched his fist and tried to swallow his anger. Mr. Pierce must have seen Turkey Vulture and Beak Nose with their loot, but he hadn't stopped them.

It is useless. Totally useless, Tag's mind screamed. *I can't do this alone, but who will help me?*

13

Tag shifted the sleeping Ferrell to a more comfortable spot on his lap. The toddler had fallen asleep in Tag's arms the instant the Model T Ford started bouncing along the dirt road toward Flagstaff. As in a horse-drawn wagon, the ride was bone-jarring, but at least the leather seat was padded.

Tag was fascinated by the inside of the convertible coupe, as he watched Dr. Colton drive. The dash was plain, except for the battery switch. There was no generator. The switch was thrown *after* the motor was started. Tag had been granted the honor of starting up the Tin Lizzie by turning the crank that protruded from the front of the car. The four cylinder engine made a distinctive but indescribable roar that Tag knew he'd never forget. The three pedals on the floorboard didn't seem to function the same as those of the cars in the future, so Tag asked Dr. Colton about them.

"This one is the brake, this one is low gear," Dr. Colton explained, "and the last one is for high gear. Takes a bit of practice to operate the gear shifts while controlling the gas feed here on the steering wheel." Dr. Colton shifted into high gear as the Lizzie picked up speed going down an incline. "Tag, would you to like to try driving her?"

"But I don't have a driver's license."

"A what?" Mrs. Colton said, looking at Tag. She sat between Tag and her husband. "I didn't know that Arizona required any kind of license in order to drive an automobile."

"Just for women, I believe, dear." Dr. Colton winked at Tag. "I can't get over how interesting the pottery sherds are that Ferrell found."

Mrs. Colton nodded. "I was thinking the same thing. Perhaps we can find a book on ancient pottery and designs."

Tag sat back listening and letting the rush of air cool him off. *One more adventure I can share with Dad: riding in a Tin Lizzie with Dr. Harold Colton and Mary-Russell Colton, discussing the ancient ones at Walnut Canyon! Why it is—or will be Dr. Colton who names the ancient ones Sinagua.*

An unnamed fear swirled around Tag. His heart lurched. *What if the Coltons don't move to Flagstaff?* Tag hugged Ferrell's cuddly body closer trying to ignore the possibility. "I really appreciate you giving me a ride into town, Dr. and Mrs. Colton."

"It is our pleasure. Your knowledge of the ancient Indians is fascinating. You are a remarkable young man." Mrs. Colton's violet perfume smelled wonderful. She reached out and caressed Ferrell's pudgy cheek. "Besides, Ferrell doesn't take to just anyone. Thank you for helping with him. I'm surprised Mr. Pierce could spare you with so many people at the canyon today."

"Oh, he won't even notice I'm gone," Tag replied. He

hadn't told Mr. Pierce he was going into Flagstaff with the Coltons. Tag's stomach flipped with a hungry flop and then knotted with the reality of the situation. Was he doing the right thing? What would Sean say and do when he just showed up on his doorstep? *I hope he still believes in not asking personal questions, like: Where did you go thirty years ago? Why haven't you aged a day since then?* Tag's mind whirled in a cycle of confusion and apprehension. But deep within, he felt he was doing the right thing in seeking Sean's help.

I'll help you anyway I can..., Sean's words spoken thirty years ago broke the circle of anxiety in Tag's mind. Yes, he was doing the right thing, the only thing he could do. The problem of destruction and pilfering at the canyon was more than just one twelve-year-old ghost boy could handle.

Tag settled back in the seat and listened to Dr. and Mrs. Colton's animated discussion of ceramic designs. Keen interest sparkled in their eyes. *They're really getting into pottery!* Tag hugged Ferrell. The sleeping child shifted and snuggled tighter against Tag. *I am definitely going to talk to Dad and Mom about a little brother when I get back.*

A wave of homesickness filled Tag's body and soul. It was a mixture of a profound longing for his mother's own loving arms and yearning for the wide-eyed, inquisitive, four-year-old, Small Cub. Tag leaned his head back against the seat and closed his eyes against burning tears.

"Thanks again for the ride." Tag jumped out of the Ford and swung his backpack onto his shoulder.

Mrs. Colton settled Ferrell in her lap. "You are more than welcome, Tag. Are you sure you can get back to the canyon?"

"Positive."

"If I didn't know better, I'd think that Sean O'Farrell and

you were conspiring to get us to move to Flagstaff," Dr. Colton said.

Mrs. Colton winked at Tag as the automobile began to roll. She called over the engine's roar, "A plot that works, I hope."

"So do I!" Tag waved, "so do I."

What will happen to the course of history if the Coltons don't move to Flagstaff? The thought again hit Tag in a wave of fear. A cold shiver crept up his back. Maybe he should go after the Coltons and do some more persuading.

"Don't worry. My pa will talk them into moving here." The young voice sounded confident to the point of being cocky.

Tag whipped around.

Sean's once-small house was now a large two-story structure with an ornate wrought iron fence surrounding it. A boy, about ten years old, with brilliant copper-colored hair and deep-blue eyes, grinned at Tag through the fence.

"Are you here to see my pa?" Reddish freckles dotted every inch of the boy's round face. The orange-gold hair was even curlier than Tag's brown hair. The boy's deep-blue, gregarious eyes were undoubtedly inherited from Sean.

"Is your dad here?"

The boy shimmied over the high fence in a fast, fluid movement and dropped beside Tag. He wore knickers, calf-length pants, and a faded cotton, striped shirt that buttoned down the front. The middle button was missing. His bare feet were a mass of freckles. "Nope. Pa's at his office." The boy inspected Tag. Curiosity danced in his eyes. "He didn't say he was expecting anyone."

"Michael T. O'Farrell is the woodbox filled yet?" A small

82

round woman in an ankle-length blue dress and a long white apron called from the front porch. White hair curled around her wrinkled but pleasant face.

"No Ma," Michael called over his shoulder. "What's your name?" he asked under his breath, still looking at his mother.

"Tag."

Michael's face whipped around, his blue eyes wide, his mouth open.

"Michael T. O'Farrell, whom are you talking to there?"

Hearing his mother's call, Michael shook himself back to reality. When he spoke, his voice sounded shaky. "Err...Ugh...just this gentleman. He needs to talk to Pa."

"Then bring him in to use the telephone to talk to Mr. O'Farrell."

"No, Ma. He has face-to-face business with Pa. I am going to take him right down to the office before Pa leaves for his trip." Michael sprang down the dirt road with catlike grace. "Come on, or Ma will put you to work splitting wood, too," he said over his shoulder.

"Michael T. O'Farrell, you come right back here after. I don't want you traipsing all over town." Tag heard Mrs. O'Farrell's Irish accent call as he ran after Michael, sprinting down the dirt road.

"Tag—that's a funny name," Michael said, slowing his pace.

Tag saw Michael scrutinizing him out of the corner of his eye. "It's just a nickname." He picked up his speed.

"You're not from around here are you?" The much-shorter Michael trotted to keep pace with Tag.

"No." The tone of Tag's voice got his message across. Michael fell silent.

After a few minutes Michael ventured, "Bet your ma doesn't make you fill the woodbox."

"Well no, actually she doesn't."

"I keep telling Pa that ten is too old to be filling the woodbox and weeding the garden. None of my five older brothers chopped wood when they were ten. They were all helping Pa at the office and all. Pa let all of them go on surveying trips when they were eight, but he won't even let me go with him on his trip today! Ma says two weeks is too long for her to have *me* gone." He shook his head. His curly hair gleamed copper in the bright sun. "It's not fair. It's just plain unfair."

Tag slowed his pace a bit. The conversation was on safer ground now. "It must be nice to have older brothers."

"Not when they're all grown and married, which means I get to do *all* the chores, which isn't fair either!" Michael peered over at Tag. "Do you know any of my brothers?"

Michael hadn't inherited Sean's trait of respecting other's privacy. Tag picked up his pace again. "No."

"Then your business must just be with Pa." Michael watched Tag out of the corner of his eye. "Must be real important business the rate you are going."

"You said your pa was leaving on a trip." Tag concentrated on the houses they passed. None of the houses existed thirty years ago. "Flagstaff has really grown," he muttered.

"Pa says that when he first built our house there wasn't a neighbor for a mile. It was just a little house then. Pa added rooms with each boy." Michael watched Tag's face. "Maybe you saw our house when it was first built."

Uneasiness churned in Tag with Michael's statement. The remark was just like the leading comments that TV lawyers would make in the future. Tag sensed more behind Michael's remarks than just a ten-year-old's curiosity. "What time is your pa leaving?"

"As soon as my brothers, Patrick and Jonathan, get back from Phoenix on the afternoon train." Michael jogged to keep up with Tag. "Come on. We'd better take the shortcut."

The shortcut sliced through an open field, across three backyards, down a road, and ended at the corner of Leroux Street and Rail Road Avenue. The railroad still ran along the south side of Rail Road Avenue, but now the many buildings on the opposite side were two-story brick buildings, instead of wood. Tag recognized some of the buildings as ones still standing in the nineteen-nineties. Horse-drawn carriages and wagons shared the rutted, dirt street with a good number of automobiles, mostly Tin Lizzies. Tag knew that this wide dirt road would be a part of the famous Route 66, the first major coast-to-coast highway. Refugees from the Dust Bowl would use Route 66 as an escape route to the promised land of southern California.

"Pa's office is just a few blocks away," Michael said, working his way through the many people on the wooden sidewalk. "Looks like the train just got in." He pointed to a large crowd of people congregated around the now sandstone depot across the street. "It's too crowded. Let's go the back way." He ducked in between two buildings and into a wide, back alley. On both sides of the alley, stacks of crates, boxes, tools, and other odds and ends leaned against the backs of the brick buildings. "It will be faster going back here." Michael hurried past a gambling hall with old tables and chairs piled high by its door.

"My pa told you to keep away from here! We don't want

you burnin' down our gambling establishment," snarled a whiny voice. A Chinese boy, smaller than Michael, sailed out from between the gambling hall and the neighboring restaurant. The nine-year-old boy, with long, blue-black hair braided into a pigtail, landed stomach first at Tag's feet with a cry. The huge, white bundle that he clutched fell open, scattering dirty tablecloths and other restaurant linen. Tag bent down to help the boy as he scrambled to gather up the spilled laundry.

An overweight boy with coarse black hair and a long, mean face swaggered toward the Chinese boy. Michael jumped in front of the Chinese boy and Tag, his feet spread apart and his fist clenched, ready to fight. "Leave Chen alone, Horse Face. Chen has every right to be here to pick up the restaurant's laundry." Horse Face was three inches taller and thirty pounds heavier than Michael, but Michael didn't seem to notice.

"So potato-eatin' Irish scum like chop suey, too," Horse Face said.

"That's because," Michael suddenly acquired a thick Irish brogue, "the Irish have brains instead of horse plop."

Horse Face lunged toward Michael.

Michael sprang to one side. Chen rolled to the other side. Horse Face's feet tripped over Chen's gyrating legs. The fat boy stumbled against Tag, toppling Tag on his back. Horse Face landed nose-to-nose on top of Tag. The air in Tag's lungs gushed out under the boy's weight. Horse Face's large brown eyes sparked anger. Tag shoved him off, trying to get to his feet. Horse Face grabbed Tag's shirttail and pulled him back. Tag swung around with his fist, but was yanked up backwards by his shirt collar.

"Leave my son alone, you stinkin' brat." Alcohol-laced breath roared into Tag's face as he was spun around by the shoulders.

Tag stared up into a fat, square face that looked somewhat familiar. "Let me go!" Tag tried to squirm away from the whiskey-barrel-round man.

The man took an awkward, limping step to counteract Tag's tugging. He shook Tag like a weed. "I'm tired of you rotten brats snooping around my..." He stopped shaking Tag and stared at him. His dark, beady eyes squinted. His mouth flopped opened. His triple chins jiggled like Jell-O. "It's— it's you! You're the little rat from Walnut Canyon!"

14

You're the dirty little kid that broke my ankle thirty years ago. Because of you, I've been a cripple all these rotten years!" Horace roared and raised his hand to strike. Tag pulled back. Michael dove against Horace's mammoth legs and bounced off to the ground. Horace tottered, cursed, and struggled to stayed on his feet.

Tag jerked away.

"Come on!" Michael cried as he flew by. Tag followed. Chen was sprinting a few feet ahead of Michael, his bundle of laundry bouncing up and down with each step.

"Go get him, Junior! Don't just stand there like a dunce. Go get that stinkin' rat!" hollered Horace.

Tag swung his head around to see Horse Face following with his flab flopping in time with his pumping legs. Tag whipped his head back around. Michael and Chen were nowhere in sight.

"Great, just great!" Tag growled, running even faster.

"Tag, Tag!" Michael's voice whispered as Tag ran past a narrow alley between two buildings.

He turned and saw Michael crouching next to a stack of wooden crates piled high against the building.

Michael waved. "Hurry!"

As Tag reached the crates, Michael disappeared behind them. "Hurry, before Horse Face sees you!"

Tag crouched down beside the crates. Michael's head and shoulders now protruded from a narrow hole at the base of the building. He disappeared into the dark opening. "Be sure and slide the crate over the entrance." He sounded like this was an everyday occurrence.

"Just shut the door behind you, he says," grumbled Tag, trying to slide the heavy crate over the low, narrow aperture. The crate slid into place and darkness swallowed everything. Tag's heart raced. "Michael!" He heard a match strike and a small light penetrated the claustrophobic darkness. Chen's and Michael's faces stared over the candle.

"Don't you know how to fight any better than that?" demanded Michael, one hand on his hip. "You'll never last a day in Flagstaff with a punch like that. Pa better teach you some good old Irish swinging and jigging." He pointed his thumb at Chen. "Tag meet Chen. He's only nine, but Chen can read better than anyone in all eight grades at school, Horse Face included."

Chen bowed from the waist. "Honored to meet you, Mr. Tag. Thank you for helping me." The shadow of the candlelight swayed and danced with his movement.

Tag bowed the best he could in the already crouched position he was in.

"You lead the way, Chen. I'll make sure he doesn't get

lost." Michael grabbed Tag's shirtsleeve. "Watch your head. When the Chinamen dug this, they didn't plan on anyone as tall as you using it."

Tag bent his shoulders over more as the tunnel's ceiling dipped lower. The candle cast just enough light to make Tag nervous. The walls of the narrow tunnel were braced here and there with lengths of lumber. The ceiling had even fewer supports than the dirt walls. Tag's palms started to sweat in the dark, cool, but stifling, air. Visions of being buried alive blurred his already poor vision. He stumbled forward and bumped into Michael. "Sorry."

"You're not afraid of small dark places, now are you?" Michael teased.

"No." Dirt pelted Tag's face as his head scraped the top of the tunnel. He brushed the dirt out of his eyes and mouth. "When was the last time the mine commission inspected this tunnel?"

"This isn't a mine! You're worse than a greenhorn," Michael snorted. "It's just an old tunnel that the Chinamen dug under the street so that they can get from one end of town to the other."

"It might be easier if they just used the sidewalks." Tag's back ached from hunching over. His chest felt like big hairy bats were flapping around in it. How could he be doing this?

"Not safe," Chen's voice came from ahead. "Too dangerous."

"This tunnel is safer? Why can't you use the streets like everyone else?"

Michael answered in an intense rush. "Prejudice is why. Plain and ugly prejudice, and I hate it. And I hate the people who keep it alive, like Horse Face and his whiskey-smelling father. The fools blame the Chinamen for the town's fires way back in 1886 and '88. If you ask me, they just want a reason to be mean." Michael yanked on Tag's sleeve. "Bigotry, pure and simple, is what it is."

Tag's feet got tangled up again. He bumped up against the side of the tunnel. Dirt trickled into his shoes. If only he could see better. No, maybe it was better if he couldn't see. He didn't want to know what was crawling or slithering in this dark hole. "How much further?"

"Not far. We're under Brannen's Store. Aren't we Chen?"

"Mr. O'Farrell's building is not far now."

"Your pa knows about the tunnel?" Tag asked.

"Oh, sure. He helped provide the lumber for the beams. He's the only white man that knows about the tunnels. Pa says he knows all about hatred and bigotry."

"Does your ma know you use the tunnels?"

"Grace be saved and heavens no, and don't you go telling her either." Michael sounded nervous. "The tunnel takes a jut to the left here. Watch your..."

Tag clunked his head. Dirt showered down around him. He gritted his teeth and stifled the scream swelling in his throat. He felt like an old man all hunched over with time. His heart raced and sweat poured into his eyes. "I can't believe I'm doing this," he muttered under his breath.

"You best stay right close or you'll stray off into one of the smaller tunnels that branch out under the other streets. You'd never find your way out. You'd spend the rest of your days wandering under the streets of Flagstaff." Tag didn't appreciate the tone of Michael's voice.

They traveled in silence for what seemed like an eternity

before Michael stopped without warning. Tag bumped into him.

Sunlight burst through the tunnel's entrance almost blinding Tag.

"Slide the crate back where it belongs," Michael instructed Tag as he emerged from the tunnel. "Hurry before anyone sees you."

Michael waved to Chen, disappearing into the back door of the building across the narrow alley. Tag couldn't read the sign over the door, written in Chinese characters. "Come on, before my pa leaves." He rushed toward a door near the crates. "Wait till Pa sees you!" The door slammed behind him.

"O'Farrell and Sons, Surveyors," Tag read the words painted on the door. His knees started shaking. *Please, Taawa let this be the right thing to do.* Tag put his hand on the brass doorknob. *Please don't let Sean ask too many questions.* He pulled the door open and slipped in.

The small back office overflowed with desks, chairs, and a long table piled with books, rolls of papers, and maps. A medium-sized man was hugging Michael, while another man sat at a desk nearby. Tag sat down in a chair close to the door. Neither of the men noticed him.

"Michael T. you look like a gopher! Where have you been?" The man ruffling Michael's dusty hair also had curly copper hair and intense blue eyes. He was in his early twenties.

"Patrick is right, Michael T.," said the other man sitting at the desk. He was the mirror image of Patrick. Both men, dressed in dark pants and white shirts, had loosened their ties. Their faces left no doubt of their devotion for their younger brother. "If you go home looking like that Ma will whomp on you good."

"I'll just sweet-talk her," Michael bragged, hoisting himself on to the desktop next to his brother. "Jonathan, you know Ma won't do nothing to me. Where is Pa?"

"He's gone. We just got here a minute ago ourselves. Train was late," Jonathan said, picking up a paper from the desk. "I was just reading Pa's letter when you came barreling in."

"Pa can't be gone! We need him."

"Relax, Michael T., and listen," said Jonathan. He began to read: "My plans have changed. I have to track someone down, and it may take a while. Meet me at the Babbitt Ranch tomorrow at ten. On your way, stop by the house for Michael T. He's going with us."

"I'm going with you. I can't believe it!" Michael cried, bounding off the desk. "I'm going for two whole weeks! No wood to chop, cows to milk, no barn to clean, no weeds to pull for two weeks!"

Tag slipped out the door without being seen. His heart felt like lead as he leaned against the closed door. Sean wouldn't be home for fourteen days. How and where could he stay for that long? Horace and his son could come looking for Michael and him any minute.

Tag checked both directions before leaving the doorway. He needed to hurry if he was going to walk back to the canyon before dark. Just the thought of the five-mile hike made Tag tired.

The door to the Chinese laundry flew open, startling Tag. Chen waved at him. "You leave?"

Tag nodded and walked on.

"Michael is not going with you?" Chen fell in pace with Tag. He had changed his tunnel-soiled pajama-like pants and long tunic top into clean ones. His scrubbed face and hands made Tag feel even grittier and dirtier. "How far you go?"

"Oh, just a couple of hundred years," Tag shrugged his shoulders and added, "I'm just walking out to Walnut Canyon."

Chen tugged on Tag's arm pulling him back toward the laundry's door. "Come. Come with me, please."

"Thanks, Chen, but I have to go. I'm in a hurry."

"I help you just like you help me. Mr. Sitgrave pick up clean laundry. Then he go to his ranch. Walnut Canyon not far from his ranch. Mr. Sitgrave very nice, has big wagon. I ask him to give you ride." Chen held the laundry door open.

15

Tag lay against the fifty-pound bags of flour and beans in the back of the buckboard. He was grateful for the ride, but even more thankful that Mr. Sitgrave suggested that he sit in the back. The thought of polite conversation overwhelmed him. His eyes closed as the wagon rocked him to sleep.

"Remember my son, the paho only has power when the moon illuminates the passageway of time," Great Owl's words roared like thunder through his uneasy slumber. He jerked straight up, panting in fear. Great Owl's warning vibrated in his drowsy mind as the wagon's endless jarring shook his body. If he waited for Sean's return, he'd have to wait an additional two weeks to go on into time. What could happen in that much time?

The wagon lurched to a stop, throwing Tag against the flour bags.

"Thanks," Tag called, watching the wagon roll away. Tag stretched out his stiff legs. It wouldn't take long to walk the half mile to the canyon. The sun hung low in the sky, and the air was cooling fast. The pine trees cast long shadows.

As Tag walked, he sorted through his thoughts and fears about staying. Could he risk staying four weeks or more? Would Horace come to the canyon looking for him? Could he keep his anger and mouth in control, or would he blow it all?

Please Great Taawa, help me know what to do, Tag prayed, *or get Great Owl to give me some help, at least.*

The roar of an automobile cut through the silence of the evening. A red sedan appeared through the trees, bumping along the rough road on its wooden wheels and narrow tires.

"I told you there wouldn't be any trouble. Old man Pierce never really checks," a man's voice boasted over the engine's noise. As the automobile passed, the two men in the front seat tipped their hats. The women in the back held huge picnic hampers.

Tag's cheeks burned. "It's useless—totally useless! No one can stop them all." He kicked a rock in his path. His toe throbbed as the rock sailed away.

* * *

Tag didn't stop at the rubble of Singing Woman's house. He forced his mind not to think about the fresh garbage and the obvious damage done that day.

A wave of homesickness crashed over Tag as he sat down in front of Great Owl's home. He leaned against the rough wall and closed his eyes. Weariness ate deep into his bones. He just wanted to climb into his own soft bed and hear his mom's loving voice telling him good night. He needed his dad to walk into his bedroom and sit down on the bed next to him. Tag ached to tell Dad all he had experienced with the ancient ones and now with the Coltons. If only he could.

"It is totally useless. I can't change a thing!" Hot tears burned his face. "I'll never get back to my own time."

Go, my son, go on into time, Great Owl's voice sang in the trees' evening song.

Goose bumps covered Tag's arms and legs. Great Owl was right. It was time to move on. He had done all he could for now. If he hurried, he wouldn't have to scale up to the cave in the dark. Tag got to his feet. He touched Great Owl's sturdy rock wall and wondered if he would ever see it in one piece again. If only just this one home could be spared.

Someone on the path behind sent Tag's heart hammering. He whirled around.

"Trumount Abraham Grotewald!" The thick brogue was unmistakable, but Sean was barely recognizable. His red hair was now white, as it poked out from beneath his black bowler. He sported a white mustache along with many distinguishing wrinkles. "When I spoke to the Coltons this afternoon, I knew it had to be you. I looked all over Flagstaff for you. When I couldn't find you there, I knew there was only one other place you could be."

Tag panicked. Sean would stop him from leaving. He sprinted up the path.

"Stop, son. I won't hurt you. You know that!"

Tag turned and waited. Sean hugged him close. "It's good to see you, son. I knew you would come back someday." Sean stepped back and adjusted his wire-rimmed glasses. "I know it's impossible, but you haven't changed a bit."

"Yes, but the canyon has," Tag's voice was tight. "I thought you, of all people, would do something to help protect it."

"I have, along with a good many others. We're doing what we can, but it takes time while..."

"While more and more vultures come to the canyon to load up baskets of artifacts and cart them off, but only after they dynamite the ruins open so they can see better!" Tag stalked off.

"I care about this canyon as much as you do, young man. The only difference is I've stayed around to help do something."

Tag whipped around. "What is the use? No one listens to me!"

"But they did, son, they did!" Sean swept up to Tag, "Major Powell and James Stevenson listened. 'Laws' you said, 'pass laws.' The Antiquities Law was passed in 1906." Sean held his broad hand up. "I know, the looting is still going on, but it's not as bad as before. You even convinced Michael Riordan. He's writing articles about Walnut Canyon and its preservation for magazines and journals all over the country." Sean put his hands on his hips. "Why there is even a Catholic priest in Flagstaff, Father Cyprian Vabre, who preaches from the pulpit that this is a holy place that shouldn't be defiled. Through the people Father Cyprian knows in Washington, including President Theodore Roosevelt himself, along with a lot of work from the rest of us, the canyon was made into a national monument."

"1915, of course," yelped Tag, grabbing Sean's arms. He danced around. "How could I be so stupid? Walnut Canyon became a national monument on November 30, 1915! But there wasn't anyone to really enforce the laws and take care of the parks and monuments except the Forest Service. And then in 1916—this year, the National Park Service was—or will be created within the Interior Department!"

Tag swirled Sean around. "With the Park Service things will change and get better *here* and in Mesa Verde, Bandelier, Chaco Canyon, Yellow..."

"What?" Sean pulled Tag to a stop. He studied Tag's face in the fading light. "I learned long ago not to question things that have no easy answers; the needless deaths, the glorious births. But boy, I have to ask. Who are you?"

"I'm just a kid who wants to be an archaeologist when he grows up—an archaeologist with something to study. I wish I could explain everything, but like you say, there are no easy answers and the answers are beyond comprehension even for me." Tag touched Sean's shoulder. "I don't know if we'll ever meet again, but I will always remember you, and appreciate what you and all the others are doing right now for the future. Thanks." Tag turned to leave, then stopped. "Sean, it's really important that the Coltons move to Flagstaff. It's more important than you can imagine. Can you work on them some more?"

Sean smiled and nodded. "From what the Coltons told me this afternoon, you've already convinced them to move here. They asked me to watch for some property for them."

"Yes! The Museum of Northern Arizona is on its way." As his cry echoed around the canyon walls Tag exclaimed, "Thanks again, Sean. Tell Michael T. good-bye for me. I've got to go now."

"Go where, son?"

Tag started up the trail. "Not where. When?"

16

Whatever *time-frame I'm in, things have improved, even though I'm freezing!* The bitter air nipped at Tag as he stood in front of Singing Woman's dwelling. He wrapped his arms around himself for warmth. The clear sky glimmered a winter crystal-blue. Tag stamped his feet to warm them. He surveyed Singing Woman's house, now clear of garbage and rubble. Much to his amazement and joy, the front wall stood, partially reconstructed. He stooped to inspect the masonry that reached his knees. *This is great. Even the mud is almost the same color as the original. Looks like whoever did this used many of the original rock slabs.*

Standing up, his head throbbed with the pain that he now knew accompanied walking time. The headache got more intense each time he regained consciousness after laying the paho on the shrine. *Maybe it hurts more the closer I get to home! Things certainly look more like 1993.*

The Island Trail had been paved, and the two hundred

and fifty cement steps leading down and around the ruins were in place. A good number of the ruins he passed were fully restored, and the garbage cleaned out of the rest. Even the graffiti scrawled on the limestone walls was gone. Gratitude warmed Tag. *I wish there were some way I could repay Sean for getting things started.*

A deep bellow shook the winter air. Tag swung around. His feet tangled up. He landed on all fours. Looking up, he saw a monstrous bull with gigantic horns charging down the path. Tag sprang up. The bull snorted and bellowed.

"Don't let him knock that new wall over!" The order came from a man chasing the bovine, waving a long stick. "Head it down the canyon! Keep it away from that wall!"

Tag could smell the animal now and see its bulging black eyes. He screamed, jumped up, and flapped his hands. The bull kept coming. Tag snatched up a rock and hurled it toward the bull. It landed short, but brought the animal to a jolting stop. It snorted and eyed Tag just long enough for him to seize another rock and sling it. Before the tennis-ball-sized rock hit its target, the bull kicked down through the bushes at the side of the trail.

"Go down after it! Head it up the canyon again on the other side of the ruins." The man wielded his stick at Tag. "Don't just stand there. Go—before it does any more damage!" The man wore pants that looked like English riding pants, tucked into his high, black leather boots. His green coat went just to his waist. A felt, flat-brimmed ranger hat covered his head.

Tag gaped at him. "But. . ."

"Go, blasted, go!"

Tag shot down the steep incline. The bull trotted along

the rocky ledge below. The animal glared back at him and bellowed. "Keep going or you'll be T-bone steak!" Tag hollered. His stomach growled at the mention of food. Small patches of snow dotted the slope. The soggy ground oozed under his jogging shoes and soaked through with freezing wetness.

"Okay, now bring him up this way," the man ordered from above, accenting each word with the stick. "We'll both get him up over the rim."

Tag scrambled around, and headed the bovine upward. The bull climbed the canyon's steep side, setting off an avalanche of rocks.

The man fell in beside Tag. "Keep him to the right."

They crested the rim of the canyon and ran into the snow-patched forest. Tag's lungs felt as though they were going to burst, and he found himself falling behind. *For a guy his age, he sure can run.*

The bull suddenly veered and started back, skirting the man. "Don't let him get back down into the canyon!"

Tag waved his arms. "Go on. Get out of here!"

The bull charged.

From out of nowhere, a rock sailed through the air. It plunked the bull on the head. A young man in a military field jacket, khaki pants, cap, and heavy military boots emerged from the trees. The teenager hurled a second rock, hitting the bull's rump as it disappeared through the trees.

"Stupid animal," he said as he approached Tag. He looked eighteen or nineteen years old. "We've built split-rail fences all around the park, but even that doesn't keep the cows out. The crazy animals knock down the ruin walls as fast as we put them up."

"Good work, boys." The man in the funny pants jogged up to them. His unzipped coat revealed a gray shirt and green tie beneath. "Daniel, where are the others?"

"They're at lunch, Ranger Beaubien, but they'll be back any minute."

"Good. Daylight is burning. The job on the newest wall looks superb." He straightened his tie and zipped up his coat, while considering Tag. "You're not on the reconstruction crew. What were you doing down in the canyon? Are you on the fencing or road crew? Well, answer."

"I'm new," Tag muttered.

Beaubien glared. "The reconstruction crew are the only ones allowed down in the canyon. There are irreplaceable antiquities in the ruins. I don't want any of you CCC Boys touching them."

"I'll see he gets to where he's supposed to be, sir," Daniel said.

"And get him back into uniform before he freezes." Beaubien spun around and marched off, his high boots sloshing through the sporadic snow. He looked over his shoulder. "We found some interesting things in the excavation yesterday. After dinner come see them, Daniel. I'll be happy to take you back to camp."

"Thanks!" Daniel waved and turned to Tag. "Don't let old Bullroar scare you. He's just real protective of things down in the canyon. Do what he says, and you'll be fine. When did you get into camp?"

"Well, I'm not really..."

Daniel nodded. "I'm sure you won't have any trouble enlisting in the CCC. You're a bit young, but I don't think they'll ask your age, seeing so many of us are leaving to fight the Germans and the Japs." He stuck out his gloved hand, "Daniel Van Ritter."

"Tag Grotewald. I hadn't really thought about enlisting. I'm just sort of passing through." His stomach growled loud and clear.

"Sounds like your belly needs to start thinking about it." Daniel slipped off his field jacket. A thick wool sweater covered most of his khaki shirt. He offered the heavy coat to Tag.

"The Civilian Conservation Corps will feed you three square meals, give you a warm place to sleep, and a dollar a day. Of course, they send twenty-two dollars a month back to your family, but the rest is yours." He peeled off his green wool gloves and handed them to Tag. "You even get clothes. They are Army issue, but they beat freezing. Maybe we can get you assigned with me. The work is hard, but it's real interesting." Daniel strolled toward the rim.

Tag followed, avoiding the piles of snow. He buttoned up the coat. It was too big, but warm. The gloves fit perfectly. "You're on the reconstruction crew?"

"Yes. I've always loved history, so working here is almost too good to be true. You must be interested in the Sinagua Indians if you came clear out here."

They reached the rim of the canyon. Tag stared down into it. "My dad is an archaeologist." Tears stung his eyes.

"Working here has made me think that's what I'd like to be too, but with six brothers and sisters back in Pennsylvania and Daddy being a coal miner, there's not much chance of me going to college." Daniel tipped his cap back on his head and studied the canyon below. A raven's harsh cry broke through the cold air. He shook his head. "The biggest reason I've stayed on here instead of enlisting after Pearl Harbor two months ago, is that I'd rather be learning about people than killing them. I'm getting to be a good mason, which is a lot better than coal mining."

Tag studied Daniel's square face with its rosy-from-the-cold cheeks. *He's too young to be fighting in a war.* How could the world be at war when everything was so peaceful and quiet here? Were boys like Daniel actually killing each other in Europe and the Pacific? A shiver shook Tag's body. He pushed the thought out of his mind. "How long have you been here?"

"Almost a year. After the first six months, I re-enlisted because I liked it so much." Daniel pointed into the canyon. "See that first ruin there under the ledge on the right? That's just one of the many I helped rebuild. It was nothing but a heap of rocks when we started. I was even lucky enough to help excavate it. It is hard, tedious work but it's like hunting for history."

His blue eyes beamed as he spoke to Tag. "We found things that are over seven hundred years old. Can you imagine? When I'd find a chunk of pottery, I'd get as excited as if it were a gold doubloon." Daniel gazed back into the canyon. "The first time I found a bone awl, I felt like I had died and gone to heaven. And you know, I feel the same way every time I find something that the Sinagua made or used. I can't keep anything I find, of course. All the things we discover go the Museum of Northern Arizona or some other museum. Have you been to the Museum of Northern Arizona?"

"Not lately." Gratitude again filled Tag. Sean had kept his word about getting the Coltons to move to Flagstaff.

"We can go into town on Saturday," Daniel said. "I

spend most Saturdays at the museum. I even know Dr. Colton and his wife, the proprietors. I'll be glad to introduce you to them. They know all about the Sinagua Indians. You'd really like them."

Apprehension surged through Tag, but he tried to hide it from his voice. "Sounds great."

"Joining the CCC has changed my life and opened up new doors for me. I feel like I've made a big difference here." He pointed down into the canyon. "Someday, I'll bring my children back here to see the walls I put up."

Tag said, "Your walls will be here hundreds of years, just like the original walls."

Daniel nodded and sank his hands deep into his pants pockets. His voice lost its excitement. "There's so much more to do here, but the camp can't stay open much longer with so many leaving to fight the war."

"What will you do when it closes?" Tag watched a raven float effortlessly in the crystal air below.

"Enlist."

A bitter wind gusted up from the canyon, stinging Tag's face. It was easy to imagine Daniel unearthing and studying artifacts and rebuilding the ruin walls, but he couldn't visualize him carrying a rifle. "Maybe you could get into an engineering unit, building things."

"Maybe."

"After the war you can go to college on the GI Bill to become an archaeologist!"

"GI Bill?" Daniel stared.

Tag gulped and sputtered. "I heard that the government is thinking about offering money to veterans for schooling, after the war of course."

"I hadn't heard that," Daniel sounded hopeful. "If they do, I can go to college and become an archaeologist like your dad."

"That would be great, Daniel. You know that there are huge ruins all over the Southwest that need excavating."

"I'd sure like to be in on a few." Daniel grinned at Tag. "Hey, let's go and get you some grub. I'll talk to the commander. He'll let you stay at the camp for a few days if you are willing to work."

"I—I don't know if..."

"The commander never turns anyone away with an empty stomach." Daniel began walking away.

Tag stared at the blue-black raven soaring. It landed on the top of a tall pine tree, swaying with the tree's dance in the breeze. Tag's stomach twisted and sang its own song to the bitter air.

Ten feet away, Daniel called, "Are you coming?"

17

It's all been too easy. Tag walked beside Daniel in the gray hues of the fading January sun. Uneasiness churned in his full stomach. He pulled the collar of the heavy field jacket tight to keep out the frigid air, as he attempted to keep up with Daniel's fast pace. Tag knew Daniel was eager to get to the temporary building that was used to catalog the artifacts found in the canyon. Daniel had obtained permission for them to leave the camp and walk back the four miles to Walnut Canyon to spend time with Ranger Beaubien. After a hearty supper at the CCC camp, they left and even hitched a ride part of the way. Now they were less than a quarter mile away from the makeshift archaeology laboratory.

Tag let his mind drift back over the afternoon's events. Now, it all seemed like a hazy dream. *It's just been too easy.*

When the commander of the CCC camp had taken his eyeglasses off to inspect him, he reminded Tag of his own grandfather. His watery blue eyes were stern, yet kind. His army uniform, unlike his dish-round face, was wrinkle-free. Short, sparse white hair lay perfectly on his head. Daniel had said the commander was about ready to retire from the military.

The commander folded his thin hands on his large desk and leaned forward. "So, young man, you want to join the CCC? I suppose Daniel filled you in on all of the details. Do you know anything about paving roads, building split-rail fences, or masonry work?"

Tag shook his head.

"But he knows all about archaeology, sir," Daniel spoke up from Tag's side. "His dad is an archaeologist."

"An archaeologist?" The commander sat upright in his straight-backed, wooden chair. The small office matched the commander—neat, organized, no frills—yet warm and comfortable.

Tag nodded again. His stomach started doing acrobatics.

"Does he know where you are?"

Shifting from one foot to the other, Tag tried to think of a truthful but acceptable answer.

The commander's eyes and voice softened. "The depression has been hard on everyone, even archaeologists. That is why President Franklin D. Roosevelt created the New Deal with all of its programs, including the CCC. There is no shame in it, son." He leaned forward in his chair. His voice took on an official sound again. "You'll have to fill out the proper forms. We'll need to know where your folks are so part of your pay can be sent to them, and it will take a few days to process it all. If you are willing to work, you can stay here till it's official." He smiled at Tag. "I can't guarantee how long this camp will be open, with the war and all, but there are other camps you can transfer to, if needed. Corporal Spier will get you the paperwork. Daniel, go get him a field jacket from the supply hut. I'll make sure they issue him the rest of the uniform tomorrow." The commander stood up and stretched his hand out.

Tag took the warm, firm hand. "Thank you, sir." He saw an unnamed sadness, or was it weariness, deep in the commander's eyes.

"Son, stay as long as you can with the CCC. You are too young to be fighting now. This war will drag on for many years, I'm afraid. There will be plenty of time for you to fight, later."

Under the cold, suspicious eye of Corporal Spier, Tag had filled out the paperwork. Spier, in his mid-twenties, hovered over Tag's shoulder like a vulture. His tenor voice twanged as he read and pointed his long, bony finger at each word. He watched everything Tag wrote down. "Seventeen? You don't look a day over fourteen, if that," he stated, when Tag filled in his age. The phone rang. Spier answered it, making his twanging voice deeper. Tag hurried to finish the forms.

On the line that required his parents' name and address, Tag wrote in his grandfather's name and farm address in Kansas. It was strange to think that his dad hadn't even been born yet. Were his grandparents even married yet? Tag fought to keep from smiling. The address would work because Grandpa grew up on the farm. Anyway, it would take at least a month or so before Spier, or anyone else, realized the error. *I'll only stay a day or two. Just to check things out*, Tag told himself while finishing the forms. He slid the completed papers across the desk to Spier. Still talking on the phone, Spier glared at him, and Tag hurried out the door.

Now, walking beside Daniel with a cold January wind whistling through the field jacket, Tag wondered if he was doing the right thing in even staying for a night. Things looked like they were going well. now. His ancient friends' homes were being restored and cared for better than anytime in the last six or seven hundred years. Why had Taawa plopped him into 1942? Or, was it Great Owl who controlled his time-walking? What was he to *do* here? Or *learn*? The thought shook Tag's mind.

"Do you think the war is going to last a long time like the commander said?" Daniel's question intruded into Tag's uneasy contemplation.

Tag answered without thought. "August 1945."

Daniel grabbed Tag's arm, pulling him to a stop. "August, 1945. How do you know?"

"I—I don't know. I'm just—just guessing." Daniel let go. Tag tried to say something, but it felt as though his racing heart blocked his windpipe. They walked in silence, the cold ground crunching beneath their feet. *When am I going to learn to think before I spout off?*

* * *

"This is the only complete piece of pottery we have found in the ruin that Daniel is rebuilding now." Ranger Beaubien, still in his ranger uniform, minus the tie, handed Tag a fist-sized bowl. They stood around a high, long table in the center of the small tin building. A strong, bare light bulb dangled on a wire from the ceiling, casting harsh shadows over the work table, where artifacts lay in boxes.

Tag held the smooth, plain brown bowl in his palm. Warmth seemed to radiate from the unimpressive bowl.

Singing Woman's wrinkled face swirled in his memory. This was her bowl, the bowl she ate stew from. Tag felt a sudden closeness to the ancient ones. A closeness that he hadn't felt since leaving the kind and loving people of so long ago. Singing Woman's soft voice seemed to whisper from the bowl. "Remember us as we were, people just as you are. Tell them our story, my speckle-faced son."

"It is really a find, considering the extent of the looting over the years." Beaubien sat down on a tall stool next to the table.

Daniel nodded. "It makes you stop and really think about the people that lived here."

"I can almost see a woman dipping her fingers into the bowl, eating corn and squash stew from it." Tag cradled the bowl and looked up at Daniel with a smile. "Of course, the grasshoppers in the stew made it crunchy."

Daniel laughed.

Beaubien rubbed his ear. "You are probably right. I'm sure that they ate anything they could find, especially to-wards the end of their stay here."

"I wonder if we will ever know why they left." Daniel took the bowl from Tag. "There are so many things we don't know about them."

"But there is a lot we do know." Tag picked up an arrow-head from a box on the table and turned it over in his hand. He knew that his hump-backed friend, Arrow Maker, had knapped the projectile with his steady hands. The stone knife Arrow Maker gave Tag still lay at the bottom of the pack on his back. "We do know that they hunted and grew crops on the rim of the canyon. They got their water from the stream at the bottom of the canyon. The ancient ones traded with people from many areas, not just from the Southwest." Tag looked at Daniel, who still cradled Singing Woman's stew bowl. "But I think most important of all, is that they were just like you and me. They laughed and cried. They had mothers, fathers, sisters, and brothers that they loved and worried about." Tears clouded Tag's eyes. "And they just wanted be happy and live in peace, too."

* * *

The days slipped by one by one. Tag didn't question why he was there but placed his trust in Taawa to guide him. He settled into the comfortable, daily routine of the CCC camp. The camp, built at the foot of Mount Elden, was four miles east of Flagstaff. The camp's seventeen portable buildings included barracks, a bathhouse, kitchen and mess hall, garage, supply hut, offices, and living quarters for the officers. Tag bunked next to Daniel in one of the four prefabricated barracks. Each day as the war engulfed the world, more bunks lay abandoned as the young men of the CCC chose to enlist to fight for their country.

Five days a week, weather permitting, Tag rode in a military truck with other young men to Walnut Canyon. At Ranger Beaubien's request, Tag was assigned to the reconstruction crew. He worked side by side with Daniel, rebuilding his friends' homes.

On snowy days, the CCC Boys stayed at the camp cleaning the barracks and doing other odd jobs. After finishing what work there was, they gathered around the small, dome-shaped radio that stood on a wooden table in the corner of the barracks. Tag found himself strangely drawn to the crackling radio that provided the entertainment and companionship that television bestowed in the future.

In the late afternoons, he enjoyed the antics of, *Jack Armstrong: The All American Boy*. In the evenings, he gathered with the others to listen to *Fibber McGee and Molly*. Everyone laughed at their shenanigans, always waiting for the moment when, much to Molly's dismay, Fibber would forget and open the door to his famous closet, and its contents spilled out in a never-ending torrent. How could he have thought television was the ultimate, Tag wondered, as the creaking door of *Inner Sanctum* lured him into a world of intrigue and suspense. How could mere words and sound effects create such vivid pictures in his mind?

The cold snowy January days stretched into an unusually warm February. Tag worked beside Daniel, rebuilding the ruins. Daniel was correct. The work was hard, but rewarding.

"Just a bit more water," Daniel stirred a mixture of sand, mud, and cement in a deep wheelbarrow with a shovel. They were on the narrow pathway in front of Singing Woman's home. "Whoa, that's enough."

Tag set the water bucket down and squatted on the ground to rest. He watched Daniel working with the thick mixture. Daniel's skill in blending the mortar to the right consistency amazed Tag. He had tried a dozen times himself to make mortar, but with little success. Now he just let Daniel have the privilege. "Just one more batch should do it, don't you think?" Tag said, studying Singing Woman's dwelling. It had taken longer than he expected to finish, due to snowy days and the extra work of restoring another ruin when its two-man crew enlisted. But now, the front wall of Singing Woman's home rose within two feet of being completed. Pride rose within Tag's chest. He, himself had built a good portion of the thick wall.

"I hope so," Daniel answered. "Ranger Beaubien said that they are ready for us to start work on the next ruin. They finished excavating it yesterday."

"You mean Arrow Maker's house?"

Daniel laughed and leaned his shovel against the wall, "You and your names. I bet you'd make up names of people who lived in every ruin here, if we let you. Your imagination is really amazing." Daniel picked up a trowel and scooped up some mortar from the wheelbarrow.

"Imagination nothing! Judging from all the stone chips they found on the ledge below the house, it is obvious that a stone knapper lived there."

Daniel reached up and spread the light-colored mortar onto the top of the unfinished wall. "You're right, of course. The way you piece things together is uncanny. Even Ranger Beaubien thinks so." Daniel picked up a flat limestone slab from the pile stacked nearby. He heaved it up and onto the mortar. It landed with a soft mushing sound. Daniel aligned the slab and scraped off the excess mortar. "You make everything here come so alive, like the old blind woman you made up. I can almost see her sitting where you are right now, weaving her yucca mats." He turned and shook his head at Tag. "And you don't think you have imagination?"

Tag picked up his trowel. Scooping up mortar with it, he said, "Most people just see the ruins, the mud-and-rock cliff dwellings. They don't really realize that the men and women living here hundreds of years ago were just like people today. People need to know that, if we are going to learn anything from the ancient ones."

"You need to come back here and be a guide after the war." Daniel scooped more mortar onto his trowel.

Tag eased a slab onto the wall. The mud squeezed out beneath and around the sides of it. He scraped off the excess mud with fast sure strokes. *The war.* The words echoed through Tag's mind.

Everything everyone did and thought about revolved around *the war.* The front page of the daily newspaper reported the war in grim details. Just last night, radio newscaster Lowell Thomas told the country that thirty-five countries were now involved in the fight against Japan, Germany, and Italy. General MacArthur's struggle to hold Bataan in the Philippines dominated all news. Each day, the number of casualties and men missing in action appeared at the bottom of the front page.

The usually noisy barracks became deadly still during the weekly radio Fireside Chats with President Roosevelt. Every young man huddled around the radio listening to the President's words. It was during these somber chats that Tag realized how desperate times were for the United States. "We will win this war and we will win the peace that follows." FDR told the nation. "We have nothing to fear but fear itself."

The war dominated conversations in the barracks. Tag knew each young man was dealing with his own decision of when to enlist. It was not a matter of whether or not to enlist, but *when.* Patriotism engulfed the country as men stood in long lines to sign up to fight for freedom, but to Tag World War II seemed so far away. It did not directly touch his life or the other CCC boys' lives in the peaceful forests of northern Arizona. Yet, Tag knew that sooner or later, each boy would trade his shovel, pick, saw, or ax for a gun. He tried to push aside the grim realization that many of these young men would die fighting for their country, before they were old enough to vote.

Tag watched as Daniel listened to the war news and the other boys discussing events. Daniel became quieter and more withdrawn around the others. He seemed torn between his fierce love of his country and his passion for the work he was doing at the canyon. Daniel only seemed relaxed and comfortable while working on the ruins or when he was with Ranger Beaubien.

Many evenings, Daniel and Tag made their way back to the canyon's laboratory and the archaeological finds of the day. Sometimes the park archaeologist, Paul Ezele, was there also. On these occasions, Daniel and Tag helped clean and catalog the artifacts. Tag wasn't sure who was learning more about the nitty-gritty work of archaeology, Daniel or himself. He only knew that they both loved learning and doing what each seemed so adept at doing. It was only during these special hours spent with Beaubien and Ezele that their thoughts were truly free of the desperation consuming the war-torn world and its people.

"How about going into Flagstaff tomorrow? There's a new Abbott and Costello movie at the Orpheum. We can go to the museum in the morning and go to a matinee in the afternoon." Daniel reached for another rock slab.

Tag stuck the tip of his trowel into the mortar. "Thanks, but I want to finish reading the new Zane Gray book I borrowed."

"I don't understand you." Daniel stared at him. "You are up to your eyeballs in archaeology, but you won't even stick your nose into the Museum of Northern Arizona, which is nothing *but* archaeology. Dr. Colton and his wife let me do all kinds of things around the museum." Daniel put his hands on his hips. "Dr. Colton probably thinks that you are a figment of my imagination. I've told him all about you, and he really wants to meet you."

I bet he does, thought Tag scraping the excess mud away from another slab. "Sorry, Daniel. I just don't feel like going to town."

I'd give anything to go to Flagstaff and the museum, Tag thought as he reached for more mortar. *But I just can't risk it. There are too many questions that have no easy answers.*

A cold chill slithered through Tag. How much longer till someone asked him the dreaded questions? When would the war deplete the CCC camp? How many more days did he have to polish his newly-acquired masonry skills? How many more hours did he have to help preserve the ancient ones' belongings? How much longer could he feel the close kinship with them that only field archaeology rendered?

Homesickness welled up within Tag's chest. How much longer till he could share what he had learned with his dad? His throat tightened. Would he ever feel his mom's loving arms around him again?

Tag sighed and closed his eyes against the threatening tears.

Questions that have no easy answers.

18

T ag read the last line of his book. Satisfied, yet wanting more, he turned the page wishing there were a few more lines. There weren't. Tag hadn't enjoyed Zane Gray in 1993, but now he couldn't read enough of him. *It's the history. I'll never look at it the same.* He laid the book down and eased out of his bunk. Standing up, his bones cracked and popped as he stretched out the kinks of the last hour of inactivity.

Stillness, except for Tag's bones adjusting themselves, filled the long, narrow building lined with bunks. Only the light directly above Tag glared against the lonely darkness of the barracks. The other boys left early in the morning for Flagstaff. Just like the last three Saturdays, the camp became a ghost town in minutes as the military bus loaded with excited CCC boys rumbled away in a cloud of dust. The officers left too, leaving only one officer to cover the camp. Even the mess hall stood empty.

The first Saturday, Tag had slept most of the day, exhausted from the strenuous work of masonry. Each Saturday since, after sleeping his fill, he went exploring around Mount Eldon's steep, rocky base. Then he read a book, or just listened to the radio. Each Saturday seemed to get longer and lonelier. He wished that he dared risk going into Flagstaff with Daniel. The fear of meeting Sean O'Farrell or the Coltons kept him trapped at the camp. Tag wondered if Sean was even still alive. Probably not, but Michael T. O'Farrell would be. At age thirty-two, was Michael T. too old to go fight? The thought of him enlisting sent coldness through Tag. He realized that his own grandfather would wade through the waters of Normandy and fight for his life on its bloody beach in 1944. Tag had heard the story once from Dad as he explained why Grandpa walked with a cane and was missing two fingers on his left hand. "Grandpa was one of the lucky ones," Dad had said.

Was anyone lucky in war? The thought tormented Tag as he stared out one of the narrow windows of the barrack. The moon's round, bumpy face stared back at him. "Is anyone lucky in war?" he asked the imaginary man.

His whispered words died in the stillness of the barracks. How many wars had the moon witnessed? How many more wars could the world endure before it was obliterated from the universe? Why couldn't men just get along with each other? *Why?* What was the purpose of it all?

He leaned his forehead against the cold window pane and peered at the moon. "Questions, questions with no easy answers," he whispered.

Overwhelming despair enveloped Tag. Homesickness churned through his depression. He just wanted to be home, safe with his mom and dad, safe in their love.

Tears clouded his view of the moon.

"Tag." The low voice came from behind.

Whipping around, Tag saw the commander walking out of the shadows. He wiped his eyes with a swipe of his cuff. "Yes, sir."

"I thought I might found you here." The commander's shoulders hunched forward a bit in his uniform. "You don't go to town much, do you?"

"No sir."

"It's just as well." The commander sat down on a bunk. He pulled out a long white envelope from his coat. "This letter came in the mail this morning."

Tag sat down on the bunk across from the commander and stared at the envelope as he opened it.

"The letter is simple enough. The Grotewalds say they don't know who you are. They sent back your first earnings." The commander held out the letter and a check.

Tag stared at the papers, his hands on the side of the bed. The barracks felt like a tomb.

"The Grotewalds are honest people," the commander said.

Tag met his eyes. "They are good people, sir."

"But they aren't your family are they?"

"They are the closest thing I have to a family now." Tears threatened as a lump worked its way up Tag's throat.

The commander nodded. He folded up the papers and slipped them back into the envelope. "I have nothing but good reports about you and your work, Tag. You can be proud of what you've accomplished here. All you CCC boys should be proud, but..." the commander stopped. His eyes looked extra watery behind his glasses. He pulled his lips tight unable to go on.

"Sir, I am sorry. I'll leave right now so you won't get into trouble." Tag bounced up. "I didn't mean to..."

The commander reached over and grasped Tag's arm with a gentle firmness. "I know, son. You've haven't caused me any trouble. Except for a few harmless pranks, none of you CCC boys have. It is wonderful to work with such fine young men in such a positive and peaceful..." the commander paused. He shook his head. "I got orders yesterday to close the camp down by the middle of next week."

Tag sunk back into the bunk. "But sir, what about the canyon and all the ruins that still need to be reconstructed?"

"It will have to wait until the war is over."

Realization hit Tag like lightning. "That means all the other boys will have to leave, too."

"They'll enlist," the commander said in short clipped words. His weariness dug deep lines around his eyes. "All of you are so young. I have a grandson not much older than you fighting in Bataan with MacArthur. Bud enlisted the day he turned eighteen, six months before Pearl Harbor. He always said that he wanted to be just like me—a military man." The commander sighed. "I've been in the military since I was fifteen. I lied about my age. My family needed the financial help, too. I rode behind Teddy Roosevelt at San Juan Hill and fought in World War One, the 'war to end all wars,' as we called it." He shook his head and paused for a moment then went on.

"Before that, I fought in the Philippines and saw American blood spilled where it is being spilled again today. I know Bud needs to be there, fighting for our very way of life here. I'm so proud of him, yet..." He closed his eyes for a minute. "Yet everyday, deep in my heart, I wish that Bud were here safe and sound with me. It is one thing to see and experience the atrocities of war and put your own life on the line, but it's quite another to have a son or grandson facing death on the battlefield."

"I think I understand, sir."

The commander smiled and nodded. "I wanted to talk to you before the others learn about the closure. There are other CCC camps that may stay open longer. I'll be happy to help find one for you."

"Thanks, sir. I appreciate it." Tag stood up. He held out his hand.

Taking Tag's hand, the commander said, "You remind me so much of Bud."

* * *

Tag ran his hand over the front wall of Singing Woman's home. In the bright moonlight, he saw each stone he had laid. Warmth filled his heart. Yes, he was proud of the work he had done. "But now, it is time to push on," he whispered, jogging up the path.

The cold wind whistled through the cave's entrance, whipping though Tag's T-shirt and blue jeans. He left his field jacket and the rest of his uniform folded neatly inside Arrow Maker's dwelling. He knew Daniel would find them there on Monday when he reported to work. A short note lay under the field jacket.

123

Dear Daniel,

I'm sorry I couldn't stay to say good-bye, but I had to leave before I changed my mind. Thanks for being such a good friend. I'm sure the commander can help you get into an engineering unit, if you ask him.

Remember the G. I. Bill when the war is over. I know you will make a great archaeologist!

> *Good Luck,*
> *T.A.G.*

Tag's icy fingers fumbled on the pack's buckles. It had taken everything he had to scale up the cliff in the moonlit night. Now, his body shook with cold exhaustion, both physical and mental.

Holding the paho over the shrine, he whispered, "Great Taawa, please guide my steps. Please, I just want to go home."

19

The scarlet sky, streaked with pink and gray clouds, draped the canyon in long, purple shadows. The warm, but cooling, air spoke of late August or early September. Tag stood on the ledge outside the cave and took a deep breath. Everything about the canyon looked, smelled, and felt like the nineteen-nineties. His head exploded with pain, and his heart raced. "I'm home!" His words fell short. Thick, deadly silence simmered around him.

His hungry stomach did a somersault. Things were too quiet, too peaceful. *The calm before the storm.* Tag pushed the sudden thought aside.

"No. Think positive. I am home." He knelt and undid the buckles on his pack. "I've got to get ready for Mom and Dad."

He pulled the things from the pack. He laid Sean's cotton shirt beside the paho. Next came his stone knife, yucca sandals, and last, the flashlight. "I wonder if the batteries in this still work after seven hundred years. What a TV commercial that would make."

Tag studied the scant pile. His sandals, knife, and the paho were the only things he had to show for the centuries of time-travel. "I'll give the sandals to Dad, but keep the knife." Tag stuck the knife into the waistband of his blue jeans. He wished he had something for his mom. *The paho?*

A chill shook his body despite the summer temperature. Now that he was back to his own time, would the paho retain its powers? *Can I still use it to walk back into time or even go in the future?* An electrical shock surged through Tag, leaving him shaking. He tried to ignore the gut-wrenching feeling that he would use the paho again, later.

The sound of a jet boomed across the sky.

Tag wrapped the paho in its buckskin. He placed it in the bottom of the pack along with the flashlight and sandals. Sean's shirt went on top. Tag slung the pack on his back and started to climb down the cliff. *I'll think about what to do with the paho later, but for now—pizza, tonight!*

The Island Trail lay deserted. "Pass closing time, which means dinner time," Tag said, sprinting along the black-topped trail. The ruins looked just like they had when he left in 1993.

He stopped at Littlest Star's metate. *Everything looks just like it did when Littlest Star stood here grinding corn. They'll never know what an accurate job they did restoring things, until I tell them!*

Tag headed for Great Owl's house. He'd stop for just a minute. He laughed. *For old times' sake!*

"Hey man, do you really think this is a good place to dig?" The voice came from below the Island Trail.

"Keep it down, Slash. Someone will hear you," answered a second voice.

Adrenaline shot through Tag.

"Sure, like who? Why do you think that I spent so much freakin' time finding out when all the Park Service pigs would be gone?"

"What if someone decided not to go to the party?"

Tag slid behind two trees growing on the side of the trail. He tried to see down over the trail, but couldn't discern who was talking. They had to be directly below, under the next strata of rocky ledge.

Slash answered, "Man, no one is going to miss that retirement bash. The guy was Chief Ranger here for a thousand years. Everyone and their dogs will be in town for it. Hey, Robert, I found something!"

Memories clicked in Tag's head. Flute Maiden had taken Walker and him into an isolated storage room to find a loincloth for him. The room had been full of huge, brownware jars and enormous storage baskets.

It was below the village. Those skunks are digging in Flute Maiden's storeroom! Tag worked his way down through the trees and boulders.

"Groovy man! Looks like this pot is huge," exclaimed Slash.

"Be careful. Go slow. If it's all in one piece, it will be worth a year's salary at the college."

Tag saw two men. He slipped behind a boulder just to the left of them.

"Hang it in your ear man, I am being careful," answered Slash. Even kneeling down, digging with a small shovel, he looked tall. He wore a faded black T-shirt with BEATLES:

MAGICAL MYSTERY TOUR, 1968, printed across the front. His brown hair looked like a cross between a bushy ponytail and a squirrel's tail. Dark sideburns melted into a scruffy, Bible-type beard. A long, wide knife scabbard hung from his leather belt, which was holding up ragged bell-bottom jeans.

Tag stiffened behind the boulder. How old was the Beatles shirt, a year or two? It didn't matter. Disappointment seeped through him—he was still a long way from his own time. He peeked around the boulder.

The other man, Robert, kneeling beside Slash, was huge. His small eyes were mere slits in his hairless, melon-shaped face. His short, black hair looked like a businessman's. A bulge of white fat rolled out from under his expensive, blue polo shirt. "I knew it! This had to be a storage room, and there has to be a lot more stuff buried here, too."

"Far out! With the full moon," Slash said, throwing a shovelful of dirt to his side, "we can dig all night and haul everything out before the Tree Pigs open up in the morning."

Robert sat back on his massive rump and wiped his sweaty face. "It'll be days before anyone comes down here, since it's off the Island Trail."

"Groovy. We can come again tomorrow since the moon will still be out enough to see by."

"Maybe, but it's risky," Robert said, digging again. "They patrol the monument pretty heavy every night."

"They're just Tree Pigs. They can't do anything!"

That's what you think, you dumb hippie, Tag fought to keep from screaming. He needed to get help.

Tag slipped through the trees and started climbing the steep incline. Rocks shot out from his shoes and rolled down. He froze.

"Hey man, what was that?"

Tag struggled up as fast as he could through the thick trees. His backpack got caught on a tree. He tugged, but the pack wouldn't budge. Tag tried to slip out of it, but it got tangled up even more. Someone was coming up the ledge below him.

Tag pulled with all his weight. A branch broke with an explosive pop. He fell flat on his face. Tag got to his knees and scooted up on all fours. The edge of the paved trail was just a foot above him. He scrambled over the ledge.

Someone grabbed his right foot.

Tag ate dirt.

"What you doing here, kid?" Slash dragged Tag down the hill toward him.

Tag flipped onto his back and kicked with his free leg. "Let me go you dirty pothunter."

Slash seized Tag's left foot and yanked. He grabbed Tag by the shoulders and lifted him up off the ground. "Shut up, you little creep."

Spit sprayed Tag's face. The smell of patchouli oil and stale body odor saturated his nose. Tag kicked. His first kick hit a thigh. The next one smashed in closer to the center. Slash doubled over, swearing.

Bear-tight arms grabbed him around the middle and started squeezing the breath out of him.

"Settle down, creep," Robert growled into Tag's ear. "I'd just as soon break you in half as look at you."

Tag couldn't get air into his lungs. His head swam and black dots blurred his vision. Tag felt himself going limp. He hit the ground, hard.

Robert stood like a giant above him. "Don't get up, or I'll kill you right now."

"Who is he? How did he get here?" Slash asked, trying to stand up straight, his face bloodless.

"He is the legendary ghost boy, for all it matters to me, but I bet I know what he's doing." Robert ripped Tag's pack off and opened it. He threw Sean's shirt on the ground and pulled out the yucca sandals. "Looks like you've been lucky tonight. These are in mint condition." He glared down at Tag. "Where did you find them?"

Tag stared back.

"What else do you have in here?" Robert pulled out the buckskin bundle and dropped the pack onto the ground.

Tag leaped up.

Slash knocked him flat. "Stay put, creep."

"It's a paho!"

"What's a paho?" Slash asked.

"A prayer stick. The Indians make pahos as offerings to the gods." Robert turned the paho over. "I've never seen one like this before. It's ancient, probably priceless. Where did you find this?"

"Answer him." Slash pulled Tag to his feet. "Where did you get it?"

Tag snapped back, "I don't know."

Slash lifted his fist.

"Don't, Slash. We don't have time to deal with him now."

"But..."

"Let's keep working while we can. When we finish, we'll take the kid with us. He'll tell us where he got these things, that is, if he wants to live." Robert put the paho and sandals back into the pack. "Go up to the truck and bring back the boxes to carry the stuff. I'll take the kid back with me." He slung the pack over his shoulder and grabbed Tag by the back of the neck. "Bring back the rope under the truck seat so we can tie him up." He pushed Tag ahead of him. "Bring the rifle, too, just in case."

"Are you sure you can handle him?"

Robert grunted. "I'll just sit on him, if I have to."

A large storage jar stood partially exposed amidst the rubble of limestone slabs. Tag could see that the two had dug in other spots before finding the jar.

Robert shoved him down on the ground. "Move and you're dead." He put Tag's pack a few yards away, next to an extra shovel and pick. Robert came back, knelt down, and started digging around the pot.

How long had it been since Slash went up the canyon—three or four minutes? *How long will it take him to get back?* Tag looked at Robert and his backpack laying just beyond him. There was no way to get the pack, but through Robert.

And no way home without the paho in my backpack!

Tag drew out his stone knife from his waistband and bolted to his feet. Robert looked up just as Tag rammed into him. It was like smashing into a ton of flab. Robert swayed, but grabbed hold of Tag.

Tag jammed the tip of his knife into Robert's hand and jerked away as the man screamed in pain. Tag stumbled backwards to the ground, but sprang back up. Robert lurched at him. Tag took off in the opposite direction, leaping over rocks and bushes. Robert huffed and puffed behind him.

Taawa, help me get away from this fat—fat, of course! Where was he? Tag tried to get his bearings as he ran. Could he find the right path?

He veered to his left and down the side of the canyon. Tag fell, and slid down the steep incline on his fanny. He got back up on his feet just as Robert started thundering down the hill.

There—there it is, the secret passage! The ancient ones had used a natural chimney up a sheer rock wall as a shortcut up to their village from below. As Walker had so aptly pointed out, it was also an escape route.

Tag's lungs felt like fire. He whipped his head around to see Robert's bright red face and huge belly flopping up and down, not far behind.

He sprinted up the narrow path that ended at a fifty-foot-high cliff. A huge, twenty-foot-long, flat slab of limestone leaned against the bottom of the cliff. It rose twelve feet, with its top resting against the cliff's face.

The entrance between the slab and the base of the cliff looked wider than Tag remembered. *Maybe this isn't going to work!* He slipped into the passage.

In the waning light of the evening, the five-foot passage-way between the slab and cliff was dim. Tag pushed through. The sides of the passage narrowed.

Yes!

After three feet, Tag had to turn sideways. His nose almost touched the cliff's base while his back rubbed the limestone slab. Tag squeezed through the last few feet.

The passage ended at the mouth of the natural chimney running up the face of the cliff. Tag heard Robert's heavy panting just outside the passage.

"You're not going to get away, creep. Come on out now!"

Tag slipped his knife into his waistband and shouted, "In your dreams." He swung himself into the shaft in the cliff. He looked up the sheer wall. His heart stopped. There was light at the top of the fifty-foot shaft, but the finger- and toe-notches chiseled up the chimney were hidden in shadows. *How can I ever make it?* His body shook with cold fear.

Robert's heavy footsteps filled the passage.

Taawa, help me! Tag reached up to the first finger-hold and pulled himself up. He fought to keep his eyes aimed up toward the opening so far above him. His hands were wringing wet with sweat. "One hand, then one foot," he panted, pulling himself up higher.

"Hey!" Robert's frightened scream echoed in the passage below. "I'm stuck! Help me, kid, I can't move!"

Tag laughed. His left foot slipped out of its hold. His laughter stopped dead as he to clung to the sheer wall. Finding the foothold again, Tag pulled himself up. *Keep going...just keep going!*

He thrust himself over the edge of the crevice and lay panting. Tag crawled away from the opening and struggled to his feet.

Got to get the paho! Tag started towards the ruins. He had to double back through the village and then down to get his backpack. Without the paho, he was doomed to stay here in the turbulent hippie age, as his dad had referred to it. Dad! Where was Dad right now? In Kansas on the farm with Grandpa growing wheat, or would he be in college? Was Dad a hippie? Tag couldn't imagine Dad with a ponytail, beard, or bell-bottom pants. Suddenly, Tag realized how little he knew about his own father's life. If he ever made it back home, he would change that!

Where is Slash? he wondered as he raced passed Great

Owl's House. He had to get down to the storage room before Slash did.

The backpack lay out in the open where Robert had thrown it. Slash was nowhere in sight. Tag sprinted out from behind a tree. The paho was there in the top of the pack. Tag exploded with hope. All he had to do was get back to the cave, and he was home free!

"Hold it right there," commanded an authoritative voice from behind him. "You are under arrest for pothunting!"

20

Tag clutched his backpack. His heart thundered in his throat. This couldn't be happening. Had he escaped from Robert and retrieved the paho, only to get arrested for pothunting?

"Drop the pack. Turn around slowly. Keep your hands where I can see them. Do it. Now!"

Tag let the pack drop, stretched his arms above his head, and turned around. The copper-haired, young man wore a flat-brimmed, Smoky-the-Bear hat and gray shirt. A gold, shield-shaped badge hung over his left shirt pocket. A small police radio was clipped onto his thick leather belt, next to an empty holster. A small revolver pointed at Tag.

The ranger, in his early twenties, started toward Tag. "You have the right to remain silent, anything you say can," he stopped a foot from Tag. "You're just a kid!" Keeping his gun on Tag, he looked around. "You're not alone are you?"

"No, but I am not..."

"Quiet!" The ranger slipped his revolver into the holster and pulled out a pair of handcuffs.

"But, there's..." Cuffs bit into his wrists as the ranger whirled him around. Tag felt his stone knife being yanked out of his waistband.

"Anything you say can and will be used against you in a court of law." The man spun Tag around to face him and demanded in a low voice, "How many others are with you, and where are they now?"

"Two, but I'm not with them. I just..."

The ranger pulled the yucca sandals out of the pack. "Then explain the knife and these sandals, and what's in this buckskin?"

"I can explain everything, but you've got to listen to me! There are two guys. The fat one is stuck in a passageway and the other..."

"Have you been smoking something funny, kid?"

"No! The other one went to get a..."

A blast shattered the air. A cloud of dust exploded three inches from Tag's feet. A second blast followed. Something whizzed passed Tag's ear and zinged off the rock ledge behind him.

"Come on." The ranger pushed Tag toward a boulder. Tag stumbled over his feet and went down. Another bullet zinged by. The ranger jerked Tag up by the handcuffs and started running with him. He pushed Tag behind the boulder. Another shot rang out.

Tag spit out dirt. The Ranger lay inches from him, his face twisting in pain as he clutched his thigh. A dark spot was soaking his green pants leg. "He hit you!" Tag sat up.

"Stay down."

"But you're going to bleed to death." Tag could see *Gary O'Farrell* on the nameplate pinned over his the ranger's right pocket.

"Your friend will blow your head off if you don't stay down."

Another bullet zinged over their heads.

"He's not my friend. I've been trying to tell you that. Where are the keys to the cuffs? If you don't let me help, we are both going to get killed." Tag met Gary's steel-blue eyes.

Gary reached into his pants pocket. "Turn over." He groaned in pain as he unlocked the cuffs. "Who are you?"

"No one interesting." Tag flipped over and slipped off his T-shirt. "Can you use your radio to get help?" From the whiteness of Gary's face, Tag was afraid that he was going to lose consciousness.

"The only person who can pick up a transmission this low in the canyon is the Park Service Dispatcher."

Tag tore off the bottom of his shirt. "Who is in town at the retirement party, right?"

"How did you know that?"

"I heard the two pothunters talking about the party." Tag pressed the strip of shirt against Gary's leg. "Why didn't you go?"

Gary spoke through gritted teeth. "The superintendent and I never got along. He didn't think that there was any need for rangers to carry guns."

The bandage was already soaking through. *He's going to bleed to death if I don't get help!* Tag tore off another strip. "If I get up higher, can some other agency, Flagstaff Police or the sheriff's department, pick up the call?"

"Possibly. But your friend will get you first."

"He's not my friend. I can get away if I crawl along this ledge and then climb up. Besides it's getting dark, that will help. Give me the radio."

"You're crazy. With a full moon tonight, there is no way you can do it."

"You'd be surprised what I can do. Give me the radio. Here take the rest of my shirt. You're going to need it." Tag traded for the radio. "By the way, are you a relative of Sean O'Farrell, the surveyor who lived here in the late 1800's, early 1900's?"

"He was my great-grandfather." Gary stared at Tag. "Why?"

Tag slipped the radio onto his waistband. "Sean fought to protect this canyon, too. You look like him, especially your eyes. Can you keep Slash away with your revolver? Good. I'll be back with help." He slithered away on his belly.

Other than the rocks scraping the skin off his bare belly, Tag had no trouble moving along the ledge. He saw the first stars poke through the darkening sky as he started up the canyon. It took only a few minutes to reach the Island Trail. The moon's bright face smiled down at him, or was it laughing at him?

"Any unit, officer down, officer down, at Walnut Canyon," Tag called into the radio as he ran up the paved trail. He leaped up the first set of steps.

I'm not high enough out of the canyon yet. He bounded up the next set of steps. Through the canyon below, a shot echoed... Two more bursts followed.

Tag's legs felt like jelly. A small revolver was no match for a high-powered rifle. Was Gary still alive?

Please Great Taawa, help him.

He pushed himself up the next five steps, repeating his call on the radio. What if no one picked up his transmission? What were the chances that anyone would be scanning the Park Service frequencies? Tag wasn't even sure if the small handset radio had the capability of transmitting more than a few miles.

"The government always buys the cheapest equipment," his dad had complained hundreds of times in frustration.

Tag felt the same frustration and fear as he climbed to another landing. He heard something moving on the trail behind him. Looking over his shoulder, he didn't see anything. Could it be Slash? Had Robert gotten himself unstuck? Tag's mind ran in mad circles.

Think, positive thoughts, he told himself as he raced up another set of steps. How many more of the two hundred and fifty steps did he have to go? In the moonlight, Tag recognized a skinny tree growing out of a huge rock. *Not far now, just around the bend and up the last four flights of steps to the Visitor Center!*

Another sound came from below. Footsteps? Tag stopped and strained to hear. Nothing but the wind rustling through the trees.

His scalp tightened. Moonlight flooded the black top trail. *I have to get off this open trail!* Tag sprinted up three steps and pushed through a clump of trees at the side of the path.

Tag's foot faltered on the steep incline. He slipped down the hill three feet, before he caught himself. He crawled up and worked his way along a narrow ledge that was closed to tourists. *If only I can just get up over the rim and into the forest, I'll have it made.*

He knew exactly where he was as he rushed up the forested trail, but hoped no one else did. Tag made the radio call again. "Officer down, officer down..."

Mr. Pierce's old ranger cabin appeared through the trees. It stood deadly quiet in the bright moonlight.

"The ghost boy is out tonight, Mr. Pierce!" panted Tag, as he raced by the house.

Tag radioed repeatedly as he ran in the direction of the Visitor Center. There was a phone outside the Visitor Center he could use. *Do they have 911 now? Probably not. I don't even have a quarter, or is it a dime?*

His legs throbbed. His lungs burned. He saw the lights of the visitor parking lot at the top of the ridge. Tag climbed.

"Where's Robert?" Slash's voice screamed through the silence of the forest. He stood at the top of the ridge, silhouetted in the strong parking lot lights. Light glinted off the rifle barrel. Tag heard the rifle's metallic action load a bullet into its chamber.

21

Tag stared at the rifle barrel. His heart beat so hard it hurt.

"Where is Robert?" Slash yelled.

"He got stuck somewhere."

"You're lying!" Slash started down toward Tag. "You're going to show me where he..." His foot stubbed a rock, and he stumbled downward. Tag swung the radio full-force into his face. The rifle went off an inch from Tag's head. A flash of white heat seared his ear.

The blast's echo rang through Tag's head as he ran into the thick pines. He couldn't even hear his own feet pounding the ground, as his mind swirled in confusion and pain. He couldn't think straight with the roar of the gun thundering in his head. *Got to get help. No, got to get away from Slash.*

Red and blue lights exploded in his eyes.

Got to keep running! He shook his head trying to clear the ringing out of his ears and the flashing lights out of his eyes.

His head throbbed with pain. Lights flashed everywhere. In confusion, Tag kept running.

Suddenly, high whining blares screamed through the sound of the gun's thunder. Looking through the trees toward the parking lot, Tag saw two, three, no four cop cars careening into the parking lot. Car doors flew open and officers barreled out, hands on their guns.

* * *

"Are you sure you know where you are going?" Snyder, a deputy sheriff, asked as Tag started off the Island Trail. The sheriff's late-forties-belly hung over his thick gun belt. Long, gray sideburns sprouted out from under his brown western hat with a Coconino County Sheriff patch on the front. Snyder had taken an instant dislike to Tag.

"Just follow him, Snyder," said a young Flagstaff policeman, named Wells. In his early twenties, he looked like a runner, lean and rugged. On his broad shoulders, he hauled a huge first aid bag. He flashed his high-intensity flashlight into Snyder's face. "You've already wasted too much time asking questions. O'Farrell is down there bleeding to death. Why can't you believe anyone younger than forty?"

"The same reason you don't trust anyone over thirty," snapped Snyder.

Tag had talked hard and fast to explain things. Only Officer Wells believed him. An ambulance was called after what seemed like an eternity. Now, the two Arizona Highway Patrolmen searched for Slash, while he led the other two officers down into the canyon.

"What were you doing here this time of night?" asked Snyder. In his flashlight's gleam, he carefully picked his way down the side of the canyon. "Doing some pothunting of your own?"

Tag didn't answer, just hurried faster. Goose bumps of cold and fear pricked his bare back and chest. Gary had to be still alive. He just had to be. *Please Taawa, let him be alive.*

"How do you know about my great-grandfather, Sean O'Farrell?" Gary asked, looking up at Tag. In the moonlight, his eyes looked like black holes in his pale face.

"Get out of the way so Wells can start working on him." Snyder grabbed Tag by the back of his neck and led him a few feet away. "I'm going back up to bring the paramedics down." His handcuffs jingled as he pulled them out.

"Don't waste time cuffing him. He's not under arrest," Wells ordered. "Get up there and get the paramedics!"

Snyder pointed at Tag. "You sit down right here on this rock, and don't you move an inch. You still have a lot of questions to answer, punk"

Tag watched Snyder climb out of sight. He hurried over to Wells, kneeling over Gary. "Is there anything I can do?"

"Pray Snyder can find his way back here." Wells' flashlight, stuck in a crook of a tree, illuminated Gary. He was unconscious.

"Is he going to be okay?" Tag knelt beside Wells.

"I'm doing everything I can, but he's lost a lot of blood, maybe too much." Wells turned his attention back to Gary.

Tag knew there was nothing more he could do for Sean's great-grandson. He picked up his backpack, walked back toward his appointed rock, and just kept going into the shadows of the night.

Only a few stars blinked. The air smelled of rain. How long had the storm been building up? Tag had been too busy dealing with Robert, Slash, and the others to notice. "Great time for a storm," he growled, looking up the face of the cliff. A cloud slipped over the moon. Tag couldn't see a foot above him.

Tears stung Tag's eyes. Weariness pressed down on his shoulders. His stomach growled in hunger. As the reality of the last hour began taking its toll, Tag shook uncontrollably and tears streamed down his face.

Thunder rolled off the San Francisco Peaks.

"I want to go home, Taawa!" Tag cried. "Please just let me go home!"

Lightning flashed through the clouds, illuminating the canyon. Thunder followed close behind.

Tag fumbled as he opened his backpack and dug around the paho and sandals for the pencil-sized flashlight. *Please let it work.* He flipped the switch. A thin, bright beam pierced the darkness. *Thank you, Taawa.* Tag slipped the pack on his back.

Lightning filled the canyon, and thunder echoed through it.

Tag aimed the beam of light up the cliff till he saw the first finger-hold just above his head. He positioned the small flashlight in his mouth and reached up to the notch, trying to aim the light so he could see.

I can't believe I am doing this!

He saw the next hold in the illumination of lightning. His neck cramped as he tried to shine the flashlight up to see the next notch.

A clap of thunder shook the air.

Goose bumps sprang up on his bare back and worked their way down his arms. He pulled himself up, feeling for the toeholds. With a high-pitched screech, something furry brushed against his cheek.

Tag screamed. The flashlight fell. His forehead banged against the limestone, as he plummeted downward.

*   *   *

He heard voices. They sounded blurred, as if they were under water. He tried to open his eyes, but they were too heavy. Every bone in his body ached, and pain seared through his head. Too tired, he slipped back into the security and warmth of nothingness.

Pizza—pepperoni and onion! The aroma was unmistakable even in his hazy, drifting state. His stomach doubled up in anticipation. He felt his mouth watering as his mind floated nowhere. Light glimmered through his closed lids, penetrating his mind. He tried to open his eyes. Lead. The fragrance of pizza attacked his nose. Far away, voices faded in an out.

"I thought you'd like some decent food, Gary."

"The pizza tastes wonderful but don't let the nurse see it, Grandpa."

"We'll make it disappear before she comes back."

He put every once of strength and concentration into forcing his eyes open. Bright lights made him shut them again. He tried to reach up and cover them, but his hand wouldn't move. The pepperoni smell was fading.

"Grandpa, do you want the last piece? I'm stuffed."

"I want it!" He managed to get the words out of his mouth somehow, or at least he thought he did. He fought against the light to open his eyes and keep them open. Things were fuzzy, like his mind. Everything had a drab green color.

His stomach flipped and flopped, hungry, yet nauseous, at the same time. His vision sharpened. An older man stood over him.

"You want some pizza?" The man had curly sandy-gray hair and a short reddish-gray beard. His steel-blue eyes were softened by bushy, reddish eyebrows.

He nodded. His forehead felt big. He tried to reach up and touch it but his arm wouldn't move. He looked down at it. A strap held it down. A clear plastic tube crawled out from a bandage on his forearm and traveled up to a plastic bottle hanging from a stand next to the bed. Panic set in. A strap held down his other arm, too.

"It's okay," the man said in a calm voice. He freed Tag's right arm. "They needed to keep your arm still so you wouldn't pull out the tubes while you were unconscious."

He looked from his arm to the man. "Where are we?"

"Flagstaff Hospital. How are you feeling?"

Before he could answer, someone said, "Grandpa, we'd better ring for a nurse. They said to let them know the minute he came around."

The man turned away to answer. "We will in just a minute, Gary. I just want to talk to him first."

He saw the other bed now. A young man with brilliant copper hair looked back at him and smiled. His face was speckled with freckles, making him look younger than he was. "Please excuse my grandfather. He's a lawyer and always needs to cross-exam everyone he meets."

"Well, this young man is going to need a good lawyer!" The man turned back to him. "I am Michael T. O'Farrell. We have met before, if I'm not mistaken. Of course, you know my grandson, Gary. Thank you for saving his hide."

He stared at the chunky man dressed in blue jeans and blue button-down shirt. The man looked at least sixty or older. His face appeared wrinkled not only by age, but by the sun. Michael T. O'Farrell seemed like the typical grandpa-type, warm and friendly, but with a definite *lawyer* air about him.

He didn't recognize Mr. O'Farrell. He shook his head. Pain rammed his brain. He touched his forehead and felt a huge bandage on it. A sick feeling replaced his hunger. He stared at Gary, lying on the other bed. It was easy to see the two men were related. Both looked at the world with the same intense blue eyes. A small, dome tent device covered Gary's leg. He wondered what happened to his leg. He looked back at Mr. O'Farrell. "I'm sorry, but I don't remember either of you."

"That's okay, son. Can you remember how you got here? No?"

"You don't remember going to get help after I was shot at Walnut Canyon?" Gary asked, leaning forward in his bed. "Or falling?"

"Walnut Canyon?" He tried to remember. Nothing came, nothing.

Mr. O'Farrell touched his arm. "Son, can you tell us your name?"

Fear curled through his mind. He tried harder to concentrate, to break through the pain zapping around in his head. Nothing came. No name. No address. No telephone number. Absolutely nothing.

Tears clouded his vision. "Who am I?"

147

22

He looked at the two pieces of wood tied together with a thin strip of leather. The eagle feathers on the thing looked decrepit. An old, beat up, canvas backpack and a pair of crude sandals lay next to the feathered stick. There was a hunk of black rock, which looked like an ancient knife, on the other side of the backpack. He studied each object on the shiny wooden desk. Nothing came to his mind, nothing.

The psychiatrist, Dr. Lance, sat behind the massive desk in a black leather chair. His middle-aged, pocked face was placid, if not bored. "You had the backpack on when they found you unconscious. Try to clear your mind totally and just focus on the items."

My mind is already clear! Empty in fact, he wanted to scream in frustration. *That's why I am here for you to help me remember something—anything.* Tears stung his eyes as he continued to stare at the three foreign objects on the desk. A gold clock on the wall ticked away the minutes.

"I know this is frightening. Your form of amnesia is unpredictable, but usually memory returns with time. One will see something, hear something, or even smell something that will stir a memory. Once that happens, other memories return also. It just takes time. It is best and safest to let time do its work and not push too hard. I thought these things might spark a memory." Dr. Lance picked up the feathered stick. "Interesting piece, isn't it? The archaeologist at Walnut Canyon claims it is an Indian prayer stick. He said that it, the knife, and the sandals are hundreds of years old. I had quite a time getting them for you to see." Dr. Lance stared at him. "The officials are eager to know where you got them."

He sat there wishing he was back in the room with Gary. At least there, he felt safe. Even in pain, Gary was kind and considerate, never asking stupid questions that just made things worse. Mr. O'Farrell smuggled in pizzas, hamburgers, and doughnuts for them. He brought blue jeans and some shirts for him, saying, "Try these on for size. We don't want you to get arrested for indecent exposure once we get you out of this place."

They were like—like family. *Family*, the word tore at him. Where was his real family? Why hadn't they come to claim him? Didn't they want him anymore? Had he done something hideous or illegal? Questions stabbed at his mind like an ice pick. The clocked ticked itself away.

Dr. Lance interrupted the clock. "Our time is up. You are lucky that Mr. O'Farrell is such a good lawyer. No one else in town could have gained custody of you for thirty days. It's fortunate that he is taking a few weeks off to get Gary back on his feet. So, I hope you will help them in any way you can.

Of course, you do feel all right about being with the O'Farrells?"

He nodded. He hadn't said more than three words in the hour *therapy session*, as they called it.

"Good. Authorities all over the country know about you." Dr. Lance peered through his horn-rimmed classes. "However, with so many runaways these days, things are more difficult. Let's hope your parents show up before the thirty days are over." He stood up and walked around the desk. "It was nice talking to you."

Leaving the psychiatrist's office, he wondered what would happen to him if his parents didn't come before the thirty days?

"Ready there?" Mr. O'Farrell asked standing behind a wheelchair. Gary sat in the wheelchair, clutching a sack of clothes and a vase of wilting flowers.

He nodded, happy to be leaving the hospital with its unpleasant smells, constant noise, impersonal atmosphere, and crummy food. Anything had to be better than this.

"Glad that you agreed to tag along with us, son." Mr. O'Farrell scratched his beard. "You know, I am partial to the name *Tag,* and the name fits you better than John Doe. What do you think?"

Tag. The name sounded hollow, but better than John for some reason. "Yea, I guess so."

"Grandpa, let's get out of here before they try and stop us," Gary said. He still looked pale and tired, but was improving daily.

"Right on!" Mr. O'Farrell wheeled the chair out. "Come on, Tag. Let's make our escape."

Tag watched the houses pass as they drove down the narrow residential streets of Flagstaff. He watched every house, read every street sign, hoping to recognize something, desperately wanting to say, "Stop! There's my house!"

Everything looked strange and irrelevant. Even the cars looked as alien as spaceships to him. It was as if someone had just plopped him into a totally new world. Nothing looked or felt familiar in the least. Tag closed his eyes, welcoming the comfortable void behind them.

Mr. O'Farrell turned the blue Bronco into a driveway. Tag saw an old, stately, two-story house surrounded by an ornate, wrought iron fence. Huge trees provided shade all round the large, impeccable yard and house.

"I need to pick up a few things here since I'm going stay with you two at the trailer. Gary, stay in the car. There is no use in you wearing out those new crutches. Tag will help me carry back what I need." Mr. O'Farrell got out of the Bronco and opened the back door for Tag.

The house smelled old, but not musty. "My father built this house. My late wife and I moved in after Father died. We raised Gary's father here." The long entry hall ended in a fancy staircase. "After he and his wife were killed eighteen years ago, we brought Gary here and raised him, too. Now, with my wife gone, too, the house is just too big for me. It will be almost cozy to stay in Gary's trailer for a while," Mr. Farrell said, climbing the steps two at a time. "It will be more convenient for him to get around in."

Tag tried to keep up with him, while looking at the old pictures hanging on the wall. Seeing them, he felt even more abandoned and alone. "Are these all your family?"

"Yes. Quite an Irish brood, isn't it?" Mr. O'Farrell stopped at the top of the stairs. He pointed to an oil painting of a man and woman. The woman's brown hair curled around her pleasant face. She sat in a chair and wore a long, blue, ruffled dress. Her hands lay on a Bible in her lap. The man, in an old-fashioned suit, stood at his wife's side. His copper hair had streaks of gray at the sides. His steel-blue eyes seemed to smile. "This is my father, Sean Michael O'Farrell. He came to Flagstaff in 1880, as a surveyor for the railroad."

Tag studied the man in the picture and then glanced over at Mr. O'Farrell. He was watching him. Tag felt uncomfortable under his intense gaze. It wasn't the first time he had caught Mr. O'Farrell scrutinizing him. Why did he get the feeling Mr. O'Farrell was playing a game of cat and mouse?

He stared back at Mr. O'Farrell. "You look more like your father than your mother."

"So they say, but I inherited my mother's overly active curiosity. Let's get going, before Gary starts laying on the horn."

Gary's trailer at Walnut Canyon was one of the government-owned trailers parked near the rim of the canyon under the ponderosa pines. The immaculate trailer had a bedroom at each end. Gary's room had a single bed and wall-to-wall books. The other bedroom had bunk beds and more books.

After getting settled down in his bed, Gary said, "Thanks Grandpa. Now stop fussing over me and let me sleep."

"Tag, are you up to some exploring?" Mr. O'Farrell said, after unpacking his suitcase.

* * *

The sky over Walnut Canyon swirled with cotton candy clouds. The air was warm with a slight breeze that carried the scent of sage, pine, and autumn.

"There are over one hundred and twenty cliff ruins built in the canyon walls." Mr. O'Farrell and Tag stood at one of the overlooks of the canyon, happy to have it to themselves. "My father said that Walnut Canyon and its ruins spoke to him like no other place on earth, except for Ireland, of course."

Tag leaned against the iron railing. The canyon looked unimpressive, just another rocky canyon. He felt Mr. O'Farrell staring at him again in that intense way. A chill spread across his shoulder blades. "How do you get down to the ruins?"

"You walk down on a paved trail. It's a good little climb. We'll do it tomorrow. Now, we best get back to check on our patient. Knowing Gary, he's probably up cleaning his revolver or mopping the floor."

They walked back through the pines in silence. Tag glanced at Mr. O'Farrell. He seemed at home in the outdoors with his jeans, cowboy boots, and denim shirt. It was hard to visualize him stuck in an office or debating in a courtroom. Who was Mr. Michael T. O'Farrell? Tag remembered him saying they had met before, or did he just dream that? The first days at the hospital were like a nightmare now.

If he knows who I am, why doesn't he just tell me? Am I so terrible or was my life so horrible that he is afraid to tell me? Tag's scalp tightened. Maybe it was better not to know.

"Questions, questions with no easy answers," Tag heard someone whisper. He looked around. Mr. O'Farrell hummed loudly as he marched along. No one else was in sight.

Who had he heard? Dr. Lance hadn't said anything about hearing voices being a part of amnesia. Was he going crazy too?

The next few days passed uneventfully. Tag helped Mr.

O'Farrell care for Gary, which was easy since he still slept a lot. The small trailer needed little upkeep. Most of the time, Mr. O'Farrell and Tag spent talking or reading. Mr. O'Farrell told Tag about his childhood in the rough western town of Flagstaff. For some reason, Tag found himself enjoying hearing about the wild and funny adventures Mr. O'Farrell recounted so dramatically. Michael T. had not been an angelic child.

Mr. O'Farrell proved to be a good listener, also, letting Tag vent his frustrations, worries, and fears, when needed. "We're here to help you, son," Mr. O'Farrell said, squeezing Tag's shoulder. "I'll do my best to keep you here with us as long as necessary."

Tag spent hours reading newspapers and magazines searching for something to jar a memory. Daily headlines reported on the escalating war in Vietnam. Students all over the country protested U. S. involvement, while each day President Nixon sent more young men to die. Young men left the country, moved to Canada to avoid being drafted. Women burned their bras for female rights. Musicians with strange names; The Beatles, The Monkeys, The Rolling Stones, and Herman and the Hermits battled for fame and fortune in the recording industry. Every picture, every article, every song on the radio drew blanks. It was all new to Tag. He remembered *nothing*.

Mr. O'Farrell and Tag went exploring around the area for short periods of time. They hiked down into the canyon and the ruins. Tag found the mud-and-rock homes interesting enough, but kept catching Mr. O'Farrell watching him as if something strange or amazing could happen any instant. It gave him the creeps.

By the fifth day, Tag needed some time alone. "Is it okay if I go sit on the rim of the canyon for a while?" He finished drying the last cereal bowl and put it in the cupboard.

"Sure. Stay as long as you want. My secretary is bringing out some legal briefs that I need to go over." Mr. O'Farrell let the dishwater out of the sink. "Just don't go too far. I'd hate to have to roust Gary out of bed to search for you."

The morning breeze had an early September nip to it. Tag sat under a tree on the edge of the canyon, watching two birds diving and dancing in the air above. Loneliness and depression filled every inch of his body. *Even those birds know who they are and where they belong. Why don't I?*

"Mind if I share the tree's shade?"

The voice startled Tag. He turned with a jerk. A stocky, young man stood behind him. His long blue-black hair blew around his lean, brownish-red face. He looked somewhere between sixteen and twenty years old. His dark almond-shaped eyes seemed to peer right through Tag, sending a chill up his back. Tag hesitated.

The young man moved beside Tag. "It's a beautiful canyon."

Tag couldn't take his eyes off the newcomer. He wore strange leather pants and a top that looked handmade. His bare feet were in beaded moccasins. He looked something like the hippie types in the magazines.

If he is, he is an Indian hippie. The strangest feeling pricked at Tag's neck. He looked away from the young man. "It's just a canyon."

"Look closer. It is a canyon wrapped in time and mystery." He put his broad hand out to shake. "I'm Walker Talayesva."

23

So what's the great mystery?" Tag asked, looking at the Indian boy sitting next to him under the pine tree at the rim of the canyon. He decided Walker Talayesva was just an Indian, not a hippie. His leather clothes weren't ornamental, but worn, from hard use. He wore a necklace. Not love beads though, just a turquoise pendant shaped like a bird, hanging on an old thin leather string. Walker was more mysterious than the canyon, especially his eyes, which were so dark brown they were almost black. When they peered at Tag, they seemed endless, timeless, yet soul-penetrating. Tag was sure secrets lay hidden within those eyes.

"The bahanas, the whites, named the ancient people that lived here *Sinagua*." Walker spoke with some sort of an accent, and he grouped his words in short phrases. "Sinagua is a Spanish word meaning *without water,* which is a good name since they didn't have much water. Their mouths thirsted always. But what did *they* call themselves?

Did they even have a name for themselves?" Walker asked.

His words brought the hair on Tag's neck up. "I'm sure they didn't have a written language, so it's impossible to know that."

"Where did they come from?" Walker paused, waiting for an answer. His eyes searched Tag's face as if he were looking into his heart.

Tag shrugged, thinking, *I can't even answer that about myself, let alone about some old, dead Indians.*

Something in Walker's eyes gave Tag the impression that he had just seen his thought. *Impossible! This guy is strung out on something.* Tag studied Walker's face. *Maybe he is a hippie after all, on a bad trip.*

The corners of Walker's mouth curved. His eyes sparkled. "Why did the ancient ones leave their cliff homes?" he asked, not breaking eye contact. "Where did they go and why?"

"Ask a Park Ranger!" Tag snapped. This guy was a real pain. He jumped to his feet and stomped off. "I've got to go."

"Questions, questions with no easy answers."

Tag swung around. "What did you say?"

"The answers are *all* here. The canyon holds all the answers."

"Who are you anyway?" Tag stood, hands on his hips, glaring at Walker. "Where did you come from?"

"I live in a village on the Hopi mesas."

"What are you doing here?"

"Like you, I'm searching for answers."

"About what?"

Walker stood up. Shorter than Tag, he looked up into his eyes. "The past, the present, and the future—isn't that what

157

we all are seeking the answers to?" He turned and walked away.

Tag watched him disappear into the thick trees, moving without a sound. Something within urged Tag to run after him, stop him, and shake him until he explained his stupid riddles. Instead, he whipped around and tromped back to the trailer. Anger and hurt churned with each step.

*   *   *

"Where are the Hopi mesas?"

Gary sat on the vinyl couch with his leg propped up on the heavy coffee table. He was up and about now, on a limited basis. Gary put down his book. "They are about ninety miles northeast of here. Actually, there are three mesas where the Hopi live. It's a reservation."

"What are they like, the Hopi?" Tag looked out the trailer window into the forest.

"Very traditional. Their pueblo villages are hundreds of years old. Going there is like walking back in time. They have religious dances, Kachina dances, which have been performed for centuries. There are four books about the Hopi on the bookshelf next to my bed, under the law books. You are welcome to read them."

Mr. O'Farrell walked in from the kitchen with a half-peeled potato in one hand and knife in the other. "Why the sudden interest in the Hopi?"

Tag squirmed in his chair. "I met someone today who mentioned them."

The next morning, Tag plopped down under the same tree. The sky was cloudless, the air comfortable. He leaned against the tree and closed his eyes. Drowsiness weighed his eyes down. The books on the Hopi Indians were so fascinating that he had read until past three A.M. Now, the buzz of bees lolled him, and the sun covered him like a blanket. He fought to keep his eyes open. The peaceful minutes flew by like a butterfly. Tag closed his eyes.

Out of the grayness of his sleep, a fragile, old man appeared. He leaned on an intricately-carved staff. His long white hair spilled over his thin, rounded shoulders. A multi-colored, beaded skullcap covered his old head. A long red kilt reached his knobby knees. His thin chest was bare, except for a fist-sized, seashell pendant. "The answers to all of your questions are here, within the walls of the canyon." His almond eyes shimmered like pools of time. "My speckled son, you must search for them." He lifted his staff at Tag. "Trust and search."

Something tickled Tag's nose. He jerked and reached up with his hand up to brush it off. A fly sang in his ear. He opened his eyes. Sunlight gleamed around the leather-clad figure standing next to him. Tag stumbled up. "Walker, I'm glad you came back. I—I—I'm sorry about yesterday." He jammed his hands deep into his pockets. "I read about your people last night. Is it true that you Hopis dance with rattle-snakes in your mouths?"

"Yes, but only the snake priests perform the sacred rite."

"Have you ever seen anyone one get bitten before?"

Walker laughed and shook his head. He cocked a dark eye brow. "Questions?"

"Yeah, I have more than my share of questions." A lump rose in Tag's throat.

"Questions with no easy answers..." Walker took a deep breath and blew it out. "We all have such questions." He

159

began walking. Tag followed. "The answers are around, if one just looks for them."

The morning grew into afternoon. Tag exhausted his questions regarding the Hopi; their ways, beliefs, and villages. Walker patiently answered them as they explored the rim of the canyon. They went full circle, and now sat under the tree where they had started.

"I'd really like to go to your village and meet your family," Tag said. His legs ached from hiking along the steep, rocky rim. With all his questions about the Hopi people, his other questions—those about himself—were forgotten. For the first time since he woke up in the hospital, he felt the fingers of depression slipping away. Life looked almost livable. "Are you going back today?"

Walker picked a blade of grass and rolled it between his fingers. "No."

"I've got to go into Flagstaff with the O'Farrells today. They are the people I'm—visiting. Maybe we can meet again tomorrow morning."

Walker smiled and nodded.

* * *

"You have a spark of spunk in your eyes." Mr. O'Farrell put a loaf of bread into the grocery cart. "I know getting out of the trailer helps. Cabin fever gets me, too. Well, we need to bring Gary into therapy every afternoon for the next few weeks. That will help."

Tag pushed the cart along. "If you don't need me, could I stay at the canyon some of the days?"

"Sure, if you'd rather be alone."

"I won't be alone," the words slipped out. Tag saw surprise, then concern spread across Mr. O'Farrell's weathered face. "I—I—well, I made a friend."

"Oh?"

"His name is Walker. He's Hopi."

Mr. O'Farrell put three cans of tuna fish into the cart. "Really?"

"He told me all about his people today. When a Hopi baby's umbilical cord falls off, the father ties it on a stick with a string and eagle feathers around it." Tag pointed to the ceiling. "He places it in the roof over the front door of their home, so the baby will always know where his heart started and where it belongs. Neat, isn't it? Of course, the traditional Hopi homes are open-beamed with natural insulation, like brush and branches woven in between the beams. Did you know that they *dragged* logs for the original roof beams from the San Francisco Peaks hundreds of years ago?"

"Can't say that I did." Mr. O'Farrell's intense eyes searched Tag's face.

"We're going to meet again tomorrow, if that's okay. You'd like Walker. You've never met anyone like him before."

Mr. O'Farrell scratched his beard. "He must be something if he can put the spunk back into you."

Walker was waiting under the tree the next morning. He stood, brushing off his leggings. "I thought the bed wouldn't let you out," he teased.

"I'm sorry. It was my turn to fix breakfast. Now, about the Indians that lived in the canyon," Tag started walking. "Do you know anything about them?"

"Oh, just a bit," Walker answered.

The pattern took root. Tag hurried in the mornings to meet

Walker. They spent the morning roaming the ruins and the forest. In the afternoons, if Tag didn't go to Flagstaff, they hiked for miles around the area. Tag felt secure, but free, with Walker, who asked no questions. Tag's worries, confusion, and frustrations abated when he was with Walker.

Only during the nights, with Mr. O'Farrell snoring in the bunk above him, did the reality of his predicament taunt him to tears. Who was he? What was his real name? Didn't his parents love him? What had he done to make them abandon him? How could the world seem completely out of sync? Why couldn't he remember anything at all? In the darkness of the nighttime, Tag kept track of the days, and prayed that Mr. O'Farrell could extend his custody rights past the thirty days. What would happen if he couldn't?

After a week, Mr. O'Farrell asked to meet Walker. Tag felt nervous with Mr. O'Farrell walking beside him through the pines. "I know you will like Walker, but...but," he stopped.

"But what?" Mr. O'Farrell asked, marching along in his usual stride.

Tag hurried to catch up with him. "Walker dresses funny, sort of like a hippie, but he's not one. He has long hair, but it's just because he's a traditional Hopi."

Mr. O'Farrell stopped and put his hand on Tag's shoulder. "Son, I don't care if his hair is sky-blue-pink and his skin is green. No one has ever accused me of being prejudiced. I just want to meet this young man who has brought you back to life."

Walker grasped Mr. O'Farrell's hand, meeting its firmness with his own. "Sir."

Tag saw a startled look on Mr. O'Farrell's face when he

looked into Walker's dark eyes. "It is nice to meet you. Tag talks about nothing else but you."

Walker laughed. "Yes, he does talk a lot, doesn't he?"

Mr. O'Farrell chuckled and shook his head. "Yes he does, but only since he met you. We'd like you to come to dinner tonight." A time was set, and Mr. O'Farrell marched off back to the trailer.

Tag knew that Walker had cast his mysterious spell over Mr. O'Farrell too. He wondered how the more cautious Gary would take to Walker.

That night, Walker and Gary discussed Walnut Canyon and its ancient people. When Gary elaborated on the artifacts found in the burial sites, Tag watched a strange sadness fill Walker's eyes. Walker stared off as if he were hundreds of miles, or years, away. Suddenly, Tag became aware that Mr. O'Farrell was scrutinizing Walker. Tag's scalp tightened.

Mr. O'Farrell escorted Walker out of the trailer at the end of the evening and didn't return for quite awhile. Warning bells went off in Tag's mind. Was Mr. O'Farrell cross-examining Walker, or was he telling Walker all about the *kid* with no past—no future?

Tag felt more alone and vulnerable than ever before. He glanced at the calendar. There were only ten days left of Mr. O'Farrell's custody. Then what would happen?

24

Tag stooped low. He placed his hands on the rock ledges at the base of the T-shaped door and half scooted, half crawled into the ruin. The pungent smell of time and decay filled his nose. The smell alone turned him off.

For the last week they had spent almost all their time in the canyon. Walker shared his view of what he thought life was like for the ancient Indians living in the cliff houses. He described pottery making, weaving, stone knapping, hunting, and even how the ancient ones plastered their walls with mud. Tag wasn't sure if Walker based his information on archaeological findings or just an overactive imagination, although, there were handprints in the mud plaster in some of the ruins. Walker came up with Indian names—Fawn, Littlest Star, Arrow Maker—for the people who lived in the cliff homes. It became a game, Walker making up such vivid details that Tag could almost see the things he described. It was interesting, fun, and a good way to keep from thinking about the void in his own life.

But, Walker kept coming back to this particular ruin. He didn't say much, just stood in the middle of the ruin as if something was going to happen. It was verging on creepiness.

Now, Walker again stood in the middle of the ruin. His shoulders slumped over, hands clenched at his side, his eyes closed.

"Walker, are you okay?"

Walker squared his shoulders, opened his eyes and smiled.

Tag plopped down on the limestone floor. "What is it about this ruin that keeps drawing you back? We've been here a dozen times in the last week."

"Your answers are *here*." Walker's normally calm voice had an edge of agitation. "Time is running out for you and for me. The others are waiting—yours for you, mine for me. Now, close your eyes. You must try to see those who lived here."

"Sometimes you are downright weird, do you know that, Walker? Okay, okay." Tag closed his eyes. The cool air felt close—stale. He peeked out of one eye. Walker clutched the pendant on his chest. His eyes clamped shut, and every inch of his handsome face strained with concentration, as if he were willing something to happen. Goose bumps spread up Tag's arm. Walker had never acted like this before. Whatever was going on, he didn't like it a bit.

Walker opened his eyes.

Tag zapped his eyes closed. "Maybe if you got me started, since my imagination is a bit dry these days."

Silence echoed around Tag. He squeezed his eyes even tighter, letting his mind free-fall.

165

Walker's voice came from an eternity away, "Five people huddle in a circle around a fire. The fire's smoke curls up the back wall and drifts along the roof and out the smoke holes above the doorway..."

Smoke tickled Tag's nose.

"A young boy holds out a bowl for some stew. His mother, swollen with child, scoops stew out the large pot on the fire."

Small Cub. The words burst into Tag's mind.

"The boy's uncle is sitting next to him..."

Tag saw a young man about nineteen, with a strong face and waist-length black hair, dressed in a loincloth. *White Badger, the Warrior Chief.*

A girl, fifteen or so, with a beautiful oval face, handed White Badger a mug. A loose, mantle-type blouse covered one of her shoulders, leaving the other bare. A short, woven skirt completed her outfit. *Flute Maiden, the medicine woman*—the words rang through Tag's mind. He knew her, somehow.

The last person around the fire emerged. It was the fragile old man with the wooden staff. *Great Owl.* He peered at Tag with dark, ageless eyes. "The answers are here, but you must..."

Tag ripped his eyes open. Sweat ran down his forehead. Ice water swelled in his veins. Pain thrashed through his head. He sprang to his feet. Fear replaced the ice water. Tag tumbled out of the low door. He gulped in the fresh, cool air. His eyes swam. *I'm going crazy!*

Sprinting, he started up the paved trail with its many steps. He needed to get out of the canyon. Tag took the stairs two steps at a time. How on earth could he have fantasized

166

those ancient people so clearly, known their names, and felt that he actually knew them? How?

"You must search, search for the answers," Great Owl's voice from came nowhere.

Tag covered his ears with his hands and leaped up the next set of steps. It was bad enough that he was hearing voices, but now he was seeing people—ancient people at that. *I've spent too much time hanging around these dumb ruins!* He tried to find a logical explanation. There had to be an explanation for the vivid people he just had witnessed. Hallucination. *No, Walker! He told me to* see *the people who lived in the ruin. Of course, it is Walker. Somehow, some way, he made me see those people. He's a witch or something!*

He collided with someone. The man was totally bald, with anchor tattoos decorating his hairy arms. The man's camera sailed to the ground. Behind the man, a hoard of tourists glared at him and blocked the trail.

Tag darted off the blacktop onto a narrow rock ledge, and made his way in front of ruins, still lying in shambles. A tree branch snagged his shirt. Ripping it free, he kept going, trying to ignore the images and sounds of ancient women chatting around T-shaped doors that no longer existed in the tumble down walls.

Cresting the rim, he ran through the trees. Where was he? He laughed. What did it matter anyway? If you didn't know *who* you were, it didn't matter *where* you where. You were still lost!

A log cabin appeared. He had walked there with Mr. O'Farrell and Walker one evening just last week. It was the original Ranger Station, and Mr. O'Farrell had told all kinds of tales about the place. Off limits to the tourists, it stood forsaken in the lengthening shadows of the late afternoon.

Out of breath, with a side ache stabbing at him, Tag collapsed on the front step of the cabin. He heard a woman's voice from behind the closed door. "That man is always sending a hungry stomach my way." Her southern accent drew each word out. "Guess he remembers his own blue belly being empty all though the War Between the States."

Tag leaped up and off the step. As he ran through the forest, a man's voice echoed through the trees. "Many people claim to have seen the ghost boy drifting in and out of the ruins after dusk. He's searching for his family who abandoned him here. Abandoned him...abandoned him..." The words ricocheted through Tag's mind like a bullet.

* * *

"Who is on your tail, Tag?" Mr. O'Farrell sat at the kitchen table with Gary.

Without an answer, Tag scrambled to the bedroom and slammed the door. *I'm going stark-raving mad!* He flopped down on his bunk and curled into a ball.

Later, Tag wasn't sure how long, Mr. O'Farrell came into the room. He felt his hands on his shoulder.

"Would you like something to eat?"

Tag curled up tighter, his face to the wall.

After a while, Gary came in and sat down on the bunk. He just sat there waiting, without saying anything. Finally he said, "Tag, let us help you." He left a while later, without Tag saying a word.

The room grew dark. Tag heard Walker's voice in the living room talking with the O'Farrells. For the last week,

Walker had come to dinner every evening. Tag crawled under the blanket and pulled it over his head. He didn't want to see Walker. In some incomprehensible way Walker was responsible for what was happening to him. He was a sorcerer or something worse. Under the light blanket, Tag curled tighter into his protective ball.

*　*　*

"You will have to go to the hearing tomorrow, Tag." Mr. O'Farrell sat down on the bed next to him. "If I can't persuade the judge to continue my custody, they'll send you to a Phoenix juvenile facility in the afternoon."

"I don't care," Tag answered without looking at him.

"Well, I certainly do. Be ready to leave at nine o'clock." Mr. O'Farrell pulled up the window blind, letting sunlight surge through the small room. He stalked out of the doorway.

Tag closed his eyes. Had it been three days since the incident at the canyon? He had lost track of day and night, not leaving the bedroom even to shower or eat. Fear kept him trapped there, fear of voices and ghosts.

I'd rather be in Phoenix. At least there aren't voices and ghosts there. Tag put his hands over his eyes. Or would the voices and ghosts just follow him wherever he went?

Tag hardly recognized Walker sitting in the back seat of the Bronco the next morning. Walker, his long hair tied at the back, wore a white, button-down shirt, blue jeans, and tennis shoes. The clothes were new. He looked like a totally different person, except for the thin leather strap of the pendant that hung around his neck and disappeared into his shirt. Tag looked into Walker's eyes—they were the same pools of endlessness.

169

Walker smiled. Tag slammed the door and stared out the window without a word. What was Walker doing there? Why was he going with them? What did Walker have to do with the custody hearing? Tag bit his lip as the Bronco left the entrance to Walnut Canyon. *Please, just don't let me see or hear anything,* he prayed silently.

Mr. O'Farrell's firm voice filtered through the closed door of the judges' chamber. Sitting on a bench just outside the door, Tag tried to make out the words. Walker sat on a bench across the narrow hallway. His eyes had that faraway gaze. Tag got the ludicrous feeling that somehow Walker was watching and listening to every word being said behind the closed door.

Tag strained harder to hear. Mr. O'Farrell's voice became louder. A voice, just as loud and firm, responded. Mr. O'Farrell's voice exploded in anger. The second voice sustained the same degree of emotion. A third voice, calmer, interrupted the escalating argument.

The door flew open and Mr. O'Farrell stomped out. His eyes looked cobalt against his angry red face. He said, "Come with me, both of you!" He marched toward the elevator door and punched the down button.

"They are idiots with horse plop for brains," Mr. O'Farrell fumed as the elevator door closed. "It's no wonder that today's young people don't trust anyone over thirty and are running away in flocks. I'd run away too with that kind of discrimination against me!"

"It's okay, Mr. O'Farrell," Tag said, staring at the closed door. "I've been enough trouble already. It doesn't matter."

"It does matter!" Mr. O'Farrell's face softened. "Tag, you're just going to have to trust us, especially Walker."

Tag cringed. He couldn't trust Walker—Walker was a witch, a sorcerer—an enemy.

The elevator door slid open to a long narrow corridor, painted bright yellow. Mr. O'Farrell hurried down the hallway. Tag trailed through the twists and turns of the hall behind Mr. O'Farrell and Walker. They were mumbling as they went. The hall ended at a strange looking, four-foot-high metal door.

Mr. O'Farrell dug into his suit coat. "It's only a ten minute recess." He pulled out a ring with a dozen keys dangling on it. "I can keep them busy for another ten or fifteen minutes at the most, so your time is limited." He put a key into the lock on the door and smiled over his shoulder. "It always pays to pick up keys when you just find them laying around." Mr. O'Farrell pushed on the door. "Walker, help me. The blasted thing is painted shut."

Walker and Mr. O'Farrell pushed together. The door sprang open. Darkness stared out of the doorway. A cold chill raced up Tag's back as he peered into the darkness of an endless tunnel. What was going on?

Mr. O'Farrell snapped open his briefcase. "Walker, here's a flashlight. Keep to the main tunnel. Side shafts branch off on each side. Count the side shafts and turn left at the third shaft." Mr. O'Farrell switched the flashlight on and handed it to Walker. "About twenty feet down that shaft on your left, you'll see light shining through a door that is ajar. Go through the door. You'll be in the basement of a camera shop. Go upstairs and out to the street. Gary is parked across the street in the parking lot."

Walker took the flashlight and held out his hand. "Thank you sir, for everything."

"I wish that I could do more, but the justice system is far from just. It's in your hands now, Walker. Good luck." He turned to Tag and pulled him into a hug and held him for a moment. "Go with Walker."

"But I don't..."

Mr. O'Farrell jerked back and looked Tag in the eyes. "You don't have any choice in the matter. You can't stay here. Son, I'd love to keep you with me, raise you up, but that wouldn't be fair to you or your parents."

"You know my parents?" Tag demanded.

"No, I don't. But judging by you, they are great people, people who deserve to get their son back."

"But..."

Mr. O' Farrell pushed Tag toward the darkened doorway. "You don't have a choice, but you do have a chance with Walker. Now go!"

Confusion and fear made things seem unreal as Tag stooped low and looked into the doorway. The flashlight barely put a dent into the all consuming darkness. What was going on?

"Come on, Tag." Walker pulled him through the door. "Watch your..."

Tag clunked his head on a pipe running along the roof of the tunnel.

"Ouch! What is this?"

Mr. O'Farrell answered, "A tunnel that the Flagstaff Electric Light Company dug in 1920, to pipe steam heat and electricity through the town. It's been out of use since 1966. Don't worry. It's safe enough. Now get going. God carry you both, wherever you walk." Mr. O'Farrell pulled the door shut.

The door closed. Darkness consumed Tag.

25

T ag's eyes adapted to the darkness. In places, his head scraped the tunnel's dirt roof. Fat and thin, insulated pipes ran at ear-level down the middle of the narrow conduit. Tag's heart raced. The air felt thick, old, unbreathable. Following Walker, he concentrated on the flashlight's thin beam piercing the darkness. They moved along the foot-wide, uneven pathway on one side of the tunnel. The tunnel's walls consisted of the rock or cement foundations of the buildings above. Rocks shifted under Tag's feet.

"When the moon lights the passageway of time..."

The words erupted in Tag's mind. He clamped his hands over his ears. "No!"

Walker turned around.

The light's beam shone into Tag's eyes. "No! Get away from me!" He took a step backwards. "Get away from me you witch!"

"Tag listen..."

"No. I won't listen to you or your voices!" He whipped around and stumbled the other way. His head hit something, and his feet twisted and rolled on rocks. "No more voices, no more people!"

Darkness swallowed him. Keeping close to the wall, with his hands out in front of him, Tag kept moving.

"Tag, wait!"

He ignored Walker's words. Mr. O'Farrell said side shafts branched out from the main tunnel. If he hurried, he could slip into one. He felt along the tunnel's rough wall, moving as fast as he dared. Unseen objects banged his head, shoulder, and shins. He stumbled and fell on the rocks, but picked himself up and spurred himself on.

Reality bled through his confusion and fear. Where was Walker? Why couldn't he see the flashlight's beam? How far had they gone before the voice started? A hundred, two hundred yards? How far had he run in the opposite direction? The wall fell away from his hand. He backtracked a few inches and followed it around into a side shaft. Tag scrambled along in the dark for minutes, or hours. He was not sure which. He stopped and listened. Nothing. Good.

"You'll never find your way out..."

"No," Tag clamped his hands over his ears.

"Spend the rest of your days wandering under the streets of Flagstaff."

Tag fell to his knees. "Stop!"

"It's okay. Tag, it's okay." Walker's voice whispered through the darkness. He sounded close.

Tag leaped up only to bang his head on a pipe. He stayed down and crawled along the tunnel's dirt floor. Rocks tore at his knees through his blue jeans.

"It's not voices you are hearing, Tag. They are memories."

"You're lying." Tag crawled faster. He didn't see the flashlight's beam anywhere, yet Walker's voice sounded just a few feet behind him. "Keep away from me!" How had Walker found him? It was so dark that he couldn't see his own nose. Noise? Of course, Walker followed the sound of his movements.

Cooler air brushed Tag's cheek. He moved toward it, hit a wall, and worked around it into another side shaft. After three or four minutes of crawling, Tag stopped and curled up against the wall. He'd wait it out. If he wasn't moving, then Walker couldn't follow unless he used the flashlight. If he saw the light coming, he'd run or something. Tag curled up tighter. Could the witch hear his pounding heart?

"They are memories. Just memories. You are not going crazy," Walker's voice whispered. "The people you saw were memories too, not hallucinations."

Tag tried to pinpoint Walker's location. He couldn't. Walker's voice wasn't coming from the left or the right. It came from everywhere, no where—from his own mind.

"The veil over your memory is falling away. Let it fall. Don't fight it. Help it."

Impossible! You're lying! Tag thought.

"Not impossible, hard to explain, but not impossible."

Walker was reading his mind! Tag put his head into his arms. It was useless. He couldn't hide from him.

"Don't be afraid of them. They are just memories. Let them come."

"Leave me alone, just leave me alone!" Tag screamed. His voice died in the darkness.

"You were in a tunnel like this once before, with two younger boys. Try to remember. Try."

Vivid images of a small Chinese boy in pajama-like clothes burst into Tag's mind. A copper-haired, freckle-faced, barefoot boy in short pants, holding a candle, stood next to him. *"You're not afraid of small dark places, are you? Best stay close or you'll wander off into one of the smaller tunnels that branch under other streets. You'd never find your way out."*

In his mind's eye, Tag saw himself following the boys as they wound along a dark passageway until a bright light burst into his mind. *"Slide the crate back to where it belongs. Hurry before anyone sees you,"* the freckle-faced boy ordered.

"It's Mr. O'Farrell," Tag whispered. "But, he's just a kid."

"That's right. Michael Tag O'Farrell was just ten years old, and you were trying to get to his father's office. His father, your friend, Sean O'Farrell, named Michael T.— Michael Tag, after you."

A man with gray hair, white mustache, wire-rimmed glasses, and bowler hat appeared in Tag's mind. He peered at Tag. *"I learned long ago not to question things that have no easy answers; the needless deaths, the glorious births. But boy, I have to ask? Who are you?"*

"I'm just a kid who wants to be an archaeologist," the Tag in his memory answered.

Tag cried out. Memories? How could all these be *his* memories? Mr. O'Farrell said his father, Sean O'Farrell, came to Flagstaff in 1880. How could he have known Sean O'Farrell? It was impossible, and there was no way he could have memories of Michael T. O'Farrell as a child. Did the T. in Mr. O'Farrell's name really stand for Tag? It was all too incredible. Tag's head throbbed with pain.

Confusion swirled around him like fog. How could this be happening?

Walker's voice came in a rush through the darkness. "You want to be an archaeologist just like your dad."

"My dad?" A man in dusty jeans, work shirt, and boots materialized in Tag's mind. The tall thin man knelt beside a trench, digging with a hand trowel. He emptied each scoop of dirt carefully into a bucket next to him.

Tag tried to see the man's face. He couldn't, yet somehow he knew this man was his father. "Dad?" he whispered. "Dad!" Tag felt a hand on his shoulder. He jumped. A feeling of warmth and security flowed into him. Serenity replaced his worry and confusion.

"He can't come to you, Tag. You have to go to him."

"But how? I don't even know who he is or where he is."

"I'll take you," Walker whispered, kneeling next to him in the dark. "But you have to help me."

"I don't understand."

"I know. You'll just have to trust me." The flashlight flipped on, pushing the darkness aside. Walker pulled Tag to his feet. "We have to hurry. Time is running out."

Tag knew he had heard Walker say that exact thing before, but when? An image of them sitting on a rocky ledge overlooking the canyon took hold of his mind. The memory faded as fast as it came. His head throbbed. Tag knew they had known each other before, and that he had to trust Walker. There was no other choice.

He followed close behind Walker. How did Walker know where he was going? The tunnel seemed an endless maze, but he moved along without hesitation.

"There it is." A strip of light seeped through a doorway.

Walker knelt and pushed the low door the rest of the way open.

Brilliant light blinded Tag. Walker grabbed his arm and pulled him down and through the doorway.

Shelves stacked with boxes lined the small basement room. A chunky man, in his late sixties, sat at a desk just inside the doorway. The man looked up from his work on the adding machine. He smiled and nodded as Walker and Tag scurried past. Walker pushed Tag up the steep stairway first.

A crowd of people swarmed the camera shop. Tag bumped into a bald man with anchor tattoos on his hairy arms. The man almost dropped his camera. "I'm sorry." Tag recognized him as the same man he had run into at the canyon. Hurrying on, he heard Walker say, "I'm glad they could fix your camera. Have a nice day, sir."

Tag burst out laughing. He rushed out the door into the bright sunlight. Why was he laughing? It wasn't funny or was it? Stress was getting to him.

A horn blared. Gary waved through the window of his red pickup truck across the street. Walker grabbed Tag's arm. "Let's go before that man makes you pay for his camera repair."

"How did you know I knocked that guy's camera down last week?"

"I saw it happen." Walker hurried into the street.

Tag stopped in the middle of the street. "You were still in the ruins. How could you have seen it happen?"

Car brakes screeched. Walker yanked on Tag. "A seer."

"Seer? What's a seer?"

"Seer. I can see that car wants you to get out of the way. Now move it."

"I thought you were lost." Gary slowed the truck, looked to the left and to the right, and ran a stop sign at the intersection.

"Lost?" Walker said, easing back into the leather seat. "Not me."

"We'll take a shortcut." Gary pulled the truck off onto a dirt road.

Tag felt Gary's tension as he drove over the rutted, dirt road. His own nerves began unraveling again. How long had they been in the tunnel? Ten, twenty or thirty minutes? Had Mr. O'Farrell been able to get continued custody, or was he now a fugitive with the authorities searching for him? Of course, that was why Gary was using the back roads! Tag looked over at Walker sitting next to the door. With closed eyes, he leaned his head against the back of the seat. He looked asleep except for the muscles straining around his jaw and down his neck.

Seer? Tag swallowed the lump in his throat. Could Walker really see things, things that others couldn't? Could he see into one's mind?

Walker chuckled, opened one eye a crack and winked.

"We've got trouble," Gary slammed on the brakes. The truck fishtailed to a stop. At the end of the road, a gold Coconino County Sheriff's car sat next to Gary's trailer. A deputy in a western hat sat behind the wheel. Gary shoved the gear shift into reverse and hit the gas. "Maybe he didn't see us." He flipped the truck around and started back down the road.

"He did." Tag watched out the back window.

"It's our friend Snyder," Gary said, looking in the rearview mirror. "No problem. He drives like an old man."

"He is an old man," Walker said calmly.

"Not far from here, there's a sharp bend with lots of foliage where you can hide. The rim isn't far from there. I'll let you out, and I'll lead Snyder away." He tromped on the gas.

"Where are we going?" Tag asked, not sure if he wanted to know.

Gary said. "Think you can find your way back?"

"No problem. Thanks for everything," Walker answered. "You'll just get a speeding ticket out of all this."

"It's more than worth it." Gary turned the steering wheel hard and hit the brakes.

Walker threw open the truck door. "Come on buddy. It's time to go walking."

Tag looked at Gary, trying to think of something to say.

"Come back and see us someday, if you can," Gary said, pushing him out. "Good luck."

Tag dashed into the trees just as the sheriff's car sped by, lights flashing.

*   *   *

Tag looked up the ten-foot, sheer cliff. "You have got to be kidding! I'm not climbing that."

"You've done it before. Just use the finger and toeholds chipped into the limestone," Walker called down from halfway up the wall.

"But, I don't remember."

"Believe me, you don't want to. Just start climbing."

Tag reached up, slipped his hand into a notch and pulled himself up. "I can't believe I'm doing this." He found the next notch. Memories flicked like a silent movie; moonlight, a flashlight stuck in his mouth, something furry against his cheek. Tag leaned in against the rough limestone, his heart pounding in his throat. This is where he had fallen, sustaining the head injury that cost him his memory. Why? What in the world had he been doing climbing this cliff at night?

"Why are we doing this?" Looking up, Tag saw Walker's face leaning out over the top of the cliff.

"Just keep moving those big feet of yours."

Tag stretched up and felt the last finger-hold. He heard footsteps on the path below. Turning his head, he saw Deputy Snyder running up the path below him. Tag heaved himself over the edge with Walker's help.

"Into the cave." Walker pushed Tag toward a narrow, dark opening.

Tag pulled back. "No way! I've had enough of dark places to last me a lifetime."

"It's not dark inside. Come on!"

"Before I go in there, you had better explain everything to me."

"We don't have time. That deputy will be up here in seconds." Walker stood in the mouth of the cave. "You are just going to have to trust me."

Tag heard Snyder swearing below. Shrugging his shoulders, he looked at Walker. "It doesn't matter anyway cause we're trapped."

"Not if we *walk time*."

"What are you talking about?" Tag moved closer.

Walker lunged and grabbed him. "Come on!" He shoved him into the cave.

Tag landed in the middle of the small cave. He tried to get back to his feet. Walker knocked him down. "Don't move." Walker rushed to the pile of rocks stacked on the ledge that jutted out of the cave's wall. He reached behind the rocks, pulled out a leather bundle and began unwrapping it. "You can either trust me and walk time with me, or stay here for good." The leather fell to the ground. Walker held a paho in his hand.

"How did you get that?"

"Great Owl made it for me, just as he made the one you had."

Tag whispered, "Great Owl, the old man with the staff."

"Yes, the seer. He watched you until he—" Walker paused. "He knew that you would need help, help that he couldn't give. He made the paho for me to walk time."

Tag's body shook. "I remember—but I don't..."

"Stay right where you are. You're under arrest," Snyder called.

Tag saw him walking toward the cave's entrance with his gun pulled.

Walker clutched the paho is his left hand. He extended his right hand to Tag, "Trumount Abraham Grotewald. Trust me. Walk time with me."

He looked at Walker—one hand extended, the other holding the paho near the shrine. Tag swung around. Snyder was just a few steps from the entrance.

"Please, Taawa, guide our steps." Tag took Walker's hand.

26

Warmth filled his cold body. Bright light beat against his closed eyelids, but Tag didn't move. Every inch of his body ached, and his head screamed in pain as he floated in and out of a dark dream. A tiny, leather loincloth, no bigger than a washcloth, was all he had on against the bitter cold. He ran through a narrow tunnel: despite his efforts, the bright light at the end of the passageway didn't get any closer.

Got to keep going. Got to get home. His legs became heavier with each stride, slowing him to cartoonish slow motion. He struggled to lift one leg at a time and swing it forward. The light he pursued pulled farther away, dimmer with each step. His frustration magnified into panic.

"Taawa! Help me. I want to go home!" Darkness swallowed the hideous images playing in his mind.

A harsh cawing pierced the darkness. Tag's head throbbed. A rock gouged into his back. He tried to move, but his body felt petrified, as if he had lain in the same spot for hundreds of years. Tag tried to open his eyes, but they felt glued shut. Pain zapped through his head with lightning force. Groaning, he forced his eyes open against the bright light.

Where am I? Tag's eyes filtered out the light, taking stock of his surroundings. *A cave?* He managed to roll from his back to his side. Cramping spasms volleyed through his body. How did he get here? Tag tried to remember, but his thoughts were mush.

Got to get up. Tag managed to get to a sitting position. Every bone in his body creaked and ached.

Sunlight bathed and refined the small cave. A natural shelf jutting out of the limestone wall was the only notable thing Tag saw. A pile of rocks lay on the shelf. *A shrine?*

A memory bobbed above his pain. *This is the cave that Dad is going to excavate.* The memory of scaling up the cliff to the cave, with lightning zapping around him, was all too real. He remembered a blinding flash of lightning hitting inches from him, and thunder deafening him as he rolled into the cave's entrance. Then what? His mind went blank.

Why had he come to the cave? He searched through the pain in his brain. Something to do with a compass—that's right. He came here to bury his Boy Scout compass for Dad to find while excavating. Pain ping-ponged against his skull. A child's small dark face, with enormous brown eyes, appeared through his pain. *Small Cub.*

Goose bumps rose up and down Tag's arms. Small Cub? Who was Small Cub? He reached up to his T-shirt pocket for his compass. The compass was gone. The pocket was gone. Tag stared at the shirt. It wasn't the hot pink T-shirt he remembered putting on this morning, but a pale yellow, button-down dress shirt streaked with dirt and dust.

"What is going on here?" Tag's words echoed around the small cave. His shoes weren't his either, but some out-dated, canvas tennis shoes without his fluorescent shoelaces. The blue jeans weren't the ones he had put on this morning.

"I must be going crazy, or maybe being so close to the lightning fried my brain." Panic drummed along with his pain. "I've got to get out of here."

Scaling down the cliff, Tag suddenly felt as if he were in a recurring nightmare. His heart hammered, his breath came in short gulps, but his feet and hands found the chiseled notches easily, too easily. The feeling that he had climbed the cliff a dozen times seized him. His head throbbed. Everything took on a nightmarish quality. If only he could think beyond the pain. There had to be a logical explanation. There always was, wasn't there?

"Questions, questions with no easy answers..." Tag's scalp tightened. Where had he heard that before?

Tag followed the path to where it forked. Confusion set in. Which way was it back to the Island Trail?

"There must be an easy way up to the ruins—I mean the village." A cold shiver snaked up Tag's back. He knew he had said those words, but when?

"What is wrong with me? The lightning's electrical current must have short-circuited my brain." Tag took the pathway leading up. "Or I am going nuts!"

He reached the crest of the Island Trail. A girl with short blond hair, about ten years old and a bowlegged man, in a colorful cowboy shirt, crawled out of one of the T-shaped doors. "It's just like walking back in time," the girl said.

"We have walked time back to when the ancient ones lived in the canyon," the words resonated in Tag's mind. A handsome,

teenage, Hopi boy, wearing an eagle-shaped pendant, shot through Tag's mind. The boy smiled. *"I am glad that you tagged along with me."*

"Let's go in this ruin," the man's voice shattered the images in Tag's mind.

"Look Dad. Someone used this big rock to grind corn on."

The bowlegged man moved next to his daughter. "You're right, whoever it was had a great view while grinding."

"It's Littlest Star's metate," the words flew out of Tag's mouth.

"Who?" The girl wore a purple, Phoenix Suns, Western Division Champions T-shirt. Her big, blue eyes stared at him.

Tag felt his face getting hot. "I—I don't know."

"Are you okay?" The man moved toward Tag.

Tag hurried up the path.

"Dad, that is the curly-headed boy on the poster that we saw at the Visitor Center. The poster said he's been missing for..."

Tag didn't hear the rest because vivid images and memories now overwhelmed him. Familiar names, faces and memories reached out from each ruin he passed. A hump-backed man, Arrow Maker, handed him a crude, but sharp, obsidian knife. *"You will earn the knife..."*

"I don't have a knife," Tag cried, hurrying on.

Three steps farther, the apparition of two rough boys formed clearly in his mind. They wore dirty overalls without shirts. *"Looks like we are just in time for lunch, Kern."*

"But first, Horace, we got a skinny skunk to kill."

Fear swept through Tag, although he didn't know anyone named Kern or Horace.

At the next T-shaped door, the apparition of a one-armed man appeared in Tag's mind. *"Come boy. You are obviously very knowledgeable about Indian artifacts..."*

A fat, round man in a blue polo shirt, sneered at him. *"He is the legendary ghost boy..."*

Tag began running—stumbling, as each memory came on top of another. Each one was clearer than the last. An ancient man, wearing a long red kilt and beaded skullcap, pointed a wooden staff at him. *"My son, now is the time for you to do that which you were sent to do."*

A young man in khaki fatigues, with a mason's trowel in hand, laughed. *"You'd make up names of people who lived in every ruin, if we let you."*

Tag ran faster.

"You are under arrest for pothunting." The copper-haired ranger aimed his revolver at him in a crystal clear memory.

"I must have been knocked unconscious or something," Tag whispered. His reason and logic battled the memories that drifted from one time period to another, one person to another with extraordinary clarity. His legs became marsh-mallows, while his stomach cramped up in a hungry, nervous knot. If only he could make it home to Dad.

Tag jerked to a stop. *Home—Dad.* The thought penetrated below his conscious level to something hidden deep within the caves of his mind. He closed his eyes. The Hopi boy appeared again.

"The veil is falling from your memory. Tag, let it fall. Trust your memories and be true to them."

Tag opened his eyes and studied the two homes nestled alone under a long ledge. A small boy's laughter drifted out of one of the T-shaped doors.

"Taawa, help me!" His own words startled him.

Taawa?

Someone was coming up the path. Tag ducked into one of the houses. An acrid smell filled his nose as memories swirled around him like thick smoke. The cry of an infant filled his ears.

Tag whirled around to the front wall. In the mud plaster, he saw the ancient handprints that he had seen a hundred times before while exploring the ruins. They were small, women's sizes. All except one pair, that looked monstrous with it's long thin fingers. A shiver ran up Tag's back. He remembered clearly the day the oversized prints had been made hundreds of years ago.

His heart thundered as Tag slipped his hand into his own print once more. The memories of walking time filled every corner of his mind, confirming what he now knew in his heart. Great Owl, Flute Maiden, White Badger, Sean O'Farrell, Major John Wesley Powell, Ranger William Pierce, Dr. and Mrs. Colton, Daniel, Michael T. O'Farrell, and Gary O'Farrell—he remembered them all in sharp detail. He had met them, talked with them, shared with them, and learned from them. Each of them had touched his life and his heart. The images of his adventures with Walker swirled in his mind.

"Walker of Time," he whispered, his hand still resting in his ancient mud print.

Walker appeared clearly in Tag's eyes and mind. Wearing his eagle pendant, a loincloth, and sandals, he stood on the rim of a pink mesa. White clouds billowed behind him. Flute Maiden stood beside him, her body swollen huge with a child about to be born. "No wonder you were in hurry to get back,

Walker," Tag said. "I told you Flute Maiden had a crush on you." Peace enveloped his heart as he saw the love in both of their eyes. "You made it home, old buddy. Home to Hopi."

Walker's voice vibrated within the ancient walls, "Remember me, remember my people. You must now see with your heart, as well as with your new sight, my friend. We still need your help." Walker's face began to fade.

"Don't leave Walker! What new sight? Tell me Walker, what new sight?" Tag cried, pressing his hand against the print in the wall with all his strength, straining to see Walker's fading face through his tears. His heart felt like it was cracking in two. "Walker, please, I just want to go ho..."

"Tag!"

His dad's loving voice reached through Tag's fears and pain, bringing him home at last.